台北PAPAGO

跟老外
介紹台北

國家圖書館出版品預行編目資料

臺北PAPAGO！跟老外介紹臺北 / 臧琪蕾著

-- 初版 -- 新北市：雅典文化，民105.11

面；　公分 -- (全民學英文；40)

ISBN 978-986-5753-73-3 (平裝附光碟片)

1. 英語　2. 讀本　3. 臺灣

805.18　　　　　　　　　　　　　105017754

全民學英文系列　40

台北PAPAGO！跟老外介紹台北

著／臧琪蕾
責任編輯／許純華
內文排版／王國卿
封面設計／姚恩涵

法律顧問：方圓法律事務所／涂成樞律師

總經銷：永續圖書有限公司

永續圖書線上購物網
www.foreverbooks.com.tw

CVS代理／美璟文化有限公司
TEL：(02) 2723-9968
FAX：(02) 2723-9668

出版日／2016年11月

雅典文化

出版社

22103　新北市汐止區大同路三段194號9樓之1
TEL　(02) 8647-3663
FAX　(02) 8647-3660

Chapter ❶ 行
Transportation

目錄

Chapter ❸ 食

Chapter 1

行

Transportation 001

PAPAGO

機場

In the Airport

Taipei is
so fun!

• Unit 1

入境

About Immigration

A: Announcement 廣播

A Ladies and gentlemen. May I have your attention, please?
廣播：各位女士先生，請注意。

We'll arrive at Taiwan Taoyuan International Airport in half an hour.
半小時後我們將抵達桃園國際機場。

The local time in Taoyuan is 14:10 p.m.
桃園當地時間是下午二點十分。

The weather is fair.
天氣晴朗。

The temperature is 83 ^{0}F.
氣溫是華氏八十三度。

Thank you.
謝謝。

Please remain seated until the airplane has come to a complete stop.

班機沒有停妥前，請您不要離開座位。

And don't forget your personal belongings.

別忘了隨身物品。

Thank you for flying China Airline.

謝謝搭乘華航班機。

And we hope to serve you again soon.

並希望很快能再次為您服務。

關鍵單字

immigration (n.)	入境
announcement (n.)	廣播
arrive (v.)	到達
local (adj.)	當地的
fair (adj.)	晴朗的
temperature (n.)	溫度
Fahrenheit (n.)	華氏
remain (v.)	保持
complete (adj.)	完整的
forget (v.)	忘記
personal (adj.)	個人的
belongings (n. pl.)	所屬物，財產

• Unit 2

海關
In the Customs

C: Customs 海關 P: Passenger 乘客

C May I have your passport and immigration card?
您的護照與入境卡？

P Here they are.
在這。

C How long will you be staying in Taipei, Taiwan?
請問在台北要待多久？

P About 7 days.
大約七天。

C What is the purpose of your visit?
您來這邊主要目的？

P I'm planning to do some sightseeing and visit some old friends.
我計畫去觀光及見見老朋友。

C Do you bring plants or food?
有任何隨身帶植物或食物？

P No, I don't.
我沒有帶任何食物進入台灣。

C Okay, have a good trip. Thank you, goodbye.
好的，祝福有美好的旅程。謝謝，再見。

關鍵單字

passport *(n.)*		護照
immigration card *(n. phr.)*		入境卡
purpose *(n.)*		目的
visit *(n.) (v.)*		拜訪
plan *(v.)*		計畫
sightseeing *(n.)*		觀光
bring *(v.)*		攜帶
trip *(n.)*		旅行

·Unit 3

換匯 (1)

Asking for Currency Exchange (Ⅰ)

C: Customer 顧客 S: Staff 行員

C Excuse me.
不好意思。

Where can I exchange money?
請問何處可兌換外幣？

S You can go to the foreign currency exchange desk.
你可以去外幣兌換處換錢。

It's over there.
就在那裡。

C What's the exchange rate for US dollar against New Taiwan Dollar?
現在美金兌台幣的匯率是多少？

S In the airport, the rate is 1:30.
在機場匯率是一比三十。

C If you are not in urgent need of money,
如果你不急著要用錢，

you can go to a current exchange center downtown.
你可以去市中心的外幣兌換處，

and have a better deal there.
那裡的價格比較好。

C Thank you.
謝謝你。

關鍵單字

currency *(n.)*		貨幣
exchange *(n.)*		交換
rate *(n.)*		匯率

004

• Unit 4

換匯 (2)

Asking for Currency Exchange (Ⅱ)

A person stands at the foreign currency exchange ceter.

有人站在外幣兌換處前面。

C: Customer 顧客 S: Staff 行員

C I'd like to change these US dollars into New Taiwan dollars.

我要將這些美金兌換台幣。

S How would you like your bills? In large bills or small bills?

你要怎麼兌換？要換成大額鈔票或是小額鈔票？

C Please give me five one-thousand-dollar notes and ten one-hundred-dollar notes.

請給我五張一千元和十張一百元的。

S Here you are.

在這邊。

C Do you accept traveler's check?
這邊可收旅行支票嗎？

S Yes, we do.
可以。

C I'd like some coins for this check.
我想換些銅板。

S No problem. May I have your passport, please.
沒問題。麻煩請您出示護照。

C Here you are.
在這裡。

And please give me a receipt.
請給我收據。

Thank you.
謝謝你。

關鍵單字

customer *(n.)*	顧客
buy *(v.)*	購買
pay *(v.)*	支付
note *(n.)*	紙幣
accept *(v.)*	接受
traveler's check *(n. phr.)*	旅行支票
coin *(n.)*	硬幣
receipt *(n.)*	收據

Unit 5

接駁車
Where is the Shuttle Bus Stop?

V: Visitor 觀光客　W: Woman 女人

V Are there any airport buses to the downtown?
請問有到市中心的機場巴士嗎？

W Yes, we have shuttle buses to the downtown.
我們有到市區的接駁巴士。

V Where is the shuttle bus stop?
哪裡有接駁公車站牌？

W At the bus pickup point of the arrival lobby in the first terminal.
在第一航廈大廳的接駁車站。

V How long does it take to ABC Hotel by the shuttle bus?
搭乘接駁車到 ABC 飯店需要多時間？

W Around one and half hour.
大約要一個半小時。

V How about taking a taxi?
如果改搭計程車呢？

W It is faster. It will take you only forty-five minutes.
計程車比較快，只要花四十五分鐘就到。

關鍵單字

visitor *(n.)*	觀光客
shuttle bus *(n.phr.)*	接駁公車
lobby *(n.)*	大廳
pickup point *(n. phr.)*	接駁站
terminal *(n.)*	航站
stop *(n.)*	站牌

火車站

In the Train Station

Taipei is so fun!

• Unit 1

台北總站 (1)
Taipei Main Station (I)

A: Amy 艾咪 M: Max 麥斯

A It's been a long time since we met last time, Max.
好久不見，麥斯。

M What a coincidence!
真巧啊！

Nice to meet you.
很高興見到你。

A What are you doing at Taipei Main Station?
今天來台北車站做什麼？

M I am just looking around.
沒事只是隨處逛逛。

關鍵單字

train *(n.)*	火車
station *(n.)*	車站
coincidence *(n.)*	巧合
meet *(v.)*	見面
around *(adv.)*	到處
look around *(v. phr.)*	隨意看看

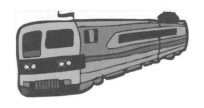

• Unit 2

台北總站 (2)
Taipei Main Station (Ⅱ)

A: Amy 艾咪　M: Max 麥斯

A Is there anything interesting here?
這裡有什麼好玩的事情嗎？

M I just went to some 3C electronic product stores and bookstores.
我剛去了一些 3C 電子賣場及書店。

A I've heard there are several food stands and a shopping center on the 2nd floor.
我聽說車站二樓上有些美食攤位還有一家購物中心。

The shopping center has been renovated and now has a new look.
購物中心剛整修過，且有新的面貌。

M It sounds great!
那真是太好了！

interesting *(adj.)*	有趣的
department store *(n. phr.)*	百貨公司
electronic product *(n. phr.)*	電子產品
stand *(n.)*	攤位
renovate *(v.)*	整修

• Unit 3

自動售票機
About Ticket Selling Machines

Mia is ready to buy train tickets by herself.
米雅正準備要買火車票。

M: Mia 米雅　V: Volunteer 車站服務志工

Ⓜ Excuse me.
不好意思。

I want to buy three train tickets to Xizhi.
我想買三張去汐止的火車票。

How do I buy tickets from the ticket selling machine?
要怎麼使用自動售票機買火車票呢？

Ⓥ You have to prepare some coins.
你要先準備好硬幣。

First, put enough amount of money.
首先，放進足額的硬幣。

When you insert enough coins for the station you are going, the light will be on.

當您放進足夠的金額時，您要去的車站按鈕，燈會亮。

Second, select the number of tickets you wish to buy.

第二步，選擇您所要的張數。

Third, choose the train type:

第三步，選擇您要搭乘的車種，

local trains, Chu-Kuang Express, or Tze-Chiang Limited Express.

區間車，莒光號，或是自強號。

Fourth, choose the ticket type:

第四步，選擇票種

full fare, half fare, old/disabled, return ticket, or child return ticket.

全票，半票，敬老愛心票，全票來回，半票來回。

Next, push the button of the station you wish to go.

接著，按下你要去的車站。

Then the tickets and changes will fall off automatically.

然後票及零錢會順勢掉下來。

You can take the tickets and go to the gate entrance.

你拿票就可以進入閘門入口。

Ⓜ Thank you for your help.

謝謝你的幫忙。

關鍵單字

ticket selling machine *(n. phr.)*	自動販售機
staff *(n.)*	職員
prepare *(v.)*	準備
select *(v.)*	挑選
fall off *(v. phr.)*	掉下
automatically *(adv.)*	自動地
entrance *(n.)*	入口

Part

3

台北捷運

Taipei Metro

Taipei is so fun!

• Unit 1

台北總站
In Taipei Main Station

S: Metro Staff 職員　P: Passenger 乘客

P Excuse me. I want to go to Taipei Main Station.
不好意思，我想去捷運台北總站。

How can I get there?
請問要怎麼走？

S Do you have any maps?
你有任何地圖嗎？

P Yes, but I only have a Taipei City map.
我只有台北市地圖。

S You can get a free map of Taipei Metro at the Information Desk.
你可以到資訊台索取免費的捷運地圖。

S A Taipei Metro map. Here you are.
台北捷運地圖，這就是囉！

First, open the map, check our location, and then find the city center.
首先打開地圖，查看我們的位置。然後尋找市中心。

You will see a special mark on the map.
你在地圖上會看到一個特殊的地標。

A building with a red roof is Taipei Main Station.
有紅色屋頂的建築就是台北車站。

Under the station building is Taipei Metro.
台北車站大樓下方即為捷運車站。

Just walk downstairs and you will see the platforms.
你走下樓就會看到月台。

You will see a lot of people waiting in line for the next train, too.
你也會看到許多人在月台上排隊等候搭乘班車。

S If you have any further questions,
如果您有任何進一步的問題，

You can check our official website on your smart phone.
您也可以透過智慧型手機查詢我們官方網站。

Just key in keywords like station names, and you will see more detailed information.
只要鍵入像站名等關鍵字，就會得到更多的詳細訊息。

If you are still confused, you can ask others for help.
要是您依然困惑，您可以請路人來幫忙。

Most Taiwanese are friendly.
大部分台灣人都很友善。

P Thank you.
謝謝。

關鍵單字

Information desk *(n. phr.)*	詢問台	
roof *(n.)*	屋頂	
mark *(n.)*	標記	
downstairs *(adv.)*	下樓地	
platform *(n.)*	平台	
wait in line *(v. phr.)*	排隊	
further *(adj.)*	更進一步的	
official website *(n.phr.)*	官方網站	
smart phone *(n. phr.)*	智慧手機	
detailed *(adj.)*	詳細的	
key in *(v. phr.)*	鍵入	
confused *(adj.)*	困惑的	
friendly *(adj.)*	友善的	

Unit 2

捷運問路
Asking for Directions

F: Foreigner 外國人　L: Local 本地人

F Excuse me. Do you know how to get to Chian Kai-Shek Memorial Hall?
打擾一下，請問如何到中正紀念堂？

L Yes. You are now at National Taiwan Normal University.
好的，你現在在台灣師範大學。

You can take Tamsui Line to the Chian Kai-Shek Memorial Hall Station.
你可以搭捷運淡水線到中正紀念堂捷運站。

Once you get off the train, just go upstairs to the Exit 5.
你下車，就直接上樓往5號出口去。

You will see it once you get out of the metro station.
一出站，你就會看到中正紀念堂站。

F Is there any interesting place to visit nearby?
附近有其他有趣的地方可以參觀嗎？

L You can go to the National Museum of History.
你可以去國立歷史博物館。

There is a special display of bronze ware and Chinese Pottery this week.
本周有青銅器與瓷器特定展覽。

It is just 10 minute walk from Chian Kai-Shek Memorial Hall.
大概從中正紀念堂走路十分鐘的距離。

F It sounds great.
聽起來很棒。

Thank you very much.
謝謝你。

L You are very welcome.
不用客氣。

關鍵單字

Chian Kai-Shek Memorial Hall *(n. phr.)*	
捷運中正紀念堂站	
National Museum of History *(n. phr.)*	
國家歷史博物館	
exit *(n.)*	出口
display *(n.)*	展示
bronze *(n.)*	青銅
pottery *(n.)*	陶器

011

• Unit 3

轉乘路線
Asking for Transfers

F: Foreigner 外國人　L: Local 本地人

F Excuse me.
不好意思。

Could you tell me how to get to the Ximen Station?
能不能告訴我怎麼搭車到西門捷運站？

L Sure! First, take the Tamsui Line to the Chain Kai-Shek Memorial Hall Station.
當然囉！你要先搭淡水線到中正紀念堂捷運站。

Then transfer to the Xiaonanmen Line and finally you will get to the Ximen Station.
再轉乘小南門線，最後就會到西門捷運站。

F So, am I at the correct platform?
那麼，我現在是在正確的月台上嗎？

L No, you should walk to the opposite platform and wait for the next train.
不是，你需要走到對面月台等下班車。

F Is this Green Line?
請問這是捷運綠線嗎？

L Yes. That's right.
是的，沒錯。

F How often does a train arrive?
多久來一班車呢？

L About ten minutes.
大約十分鐘。

F I see. Thank you.
我了解了。謝謝。

關鍵單字

transfer *(v.)*	轉乘
opposite *(adj.)*	對面的
platform *(n.)*	月台

012

·Unit 4

票價
Asking for Ticket Fares

B: Backpacker 背包客 C: Counter 櫃台

B Hello, I'd like to go to Taipei Zoo.
你好，我想去動物園。

How much is the ticket to Taipei Zoo?
請問到動物園的票價要多少錢？

C One way ticket costs NT $35.
單程票是新台幣三十五元整。

If you travel by an Easy Card, you'll get some discounts.
假如使用悠遊卡，你可以得到一些折扣。

B How much discount can I get?
折扣有多少？

C Three dollars.
三塊錢台幣。

That is, you just have to pay NT $32 for your one way trip to Taipei Zoo.

也就是，你只需付新台幣三十二元整。

B How much does an Easy Card cost?

悠遊卡一張票多少錢？

C It costs NT$200, including NT$100 deposit.

二百元，內含一百元押金。

B Well, I will buy a one-way ticket for an adult.

買一張單程成人車票。

C Here you are.

車票在這裡。

It costs NT$35 .

一共三十五元。

Have a good day.

祝你今日愉快。

關鍵單字

Easy Card *(n. phr.)*	悠遊卡
one way ticket *(n. phr.)*	單程車票
discount *(v.) (n.)*	折扣
cost *(v.)*	花費
trip *(n.)*	車程，行程
that is *(adv. phr.)*	換句話說
deposit *(n.)*	押金

題外話: ● ● ● ●

台幣的說法：

1949 年新台幣正式啟用，英文名稱為 New Taiwan dollar，常縮寫為 NT dollar，所以台幣 35 元的口語表達為 thirty-five New Taiwan dollars。在確認對方知道討論的幣值是台幣之後，對話裡可以直接說 thirty-five dollars，或是直接說 thirty-five，而不用一直重複冗長的 New Taiwan dollars。另外，簡易的英文縮寫方式有 NT、NTD、NT$、TWD (Taiwanese dollar)。

013

• Unit 5

捷運自動售票機
About Ticket Selling Machines

Mia is ready to buy MRT tickets from a ticket selling machine.
米雅正準備要從捷運自動售票機買票。

M: Mia 米雅 L: Local 當地民眾

M Hello, I am going to Tamsui.
我想去淡水。

How can I get tickets from the machine?
我要怎麼從機器買票？

L No problem. Let me show you.
沒問題，我示範給你看。

First, you have to read the route map, find the Tamsui Station.
首先，你要先讀路線圖，找到淡水站，

And select the ticket price on the touch screen.
然後在觸控螢幕選擇票價。

Then, choose the number of tickets you want to buy.

選擇你要的張數。

M Well, I just need one ticket.

嗯，我只要買一張票。

L Okay, and then insert the coins.

好的，然後投入硬幣。

The ticket coin will drop automatically.

硬枚票幣會自動掉下來。

See! Here you are!

喏，這是你的票幣。

M Thanks.

多謝啦。

But I am wondering why you have different ticket rates?

但我好奇為什麼每張票不同票價呢？

L The ticket rates are based on the distance from the station where you depart.

票價是根據你距離你出發站的遠近來計算。

The range is from 20 dollars to 65 dollars.

票價範圍從二十元整至六十五整不等。

關鍵單字

route *(n.)*	路徑，路線
drop *(v.)*	掉落
rate *(n.)*	費率
distance *(n.)*	距離
range *(n.)*	範圍
touch screen *(n. phr.)*	觸控螢幕

014

• Unit 6

詢問規定
Asking for Regulations

P: Passenger 乘客　L: Local 當地民眾

P Are there any special regulations in a metro station?
請問捷運站有什麼特殊規定嗎？

L You see there's a yellow line on the floor.
你看一下，地面上有一條黃色線。

Behind the yellow line, smoking, spitting betel nut juice, and chewing gum are not allowed.
黃色線之後，禁止抽菸吐檳榔汁與吃口香糖。

Moreover, littering cigarette butts, drinking and eating are not allowed, either.
還有丟菸蒂和喝飲料也是不予許的。

P Do I have to buy tickets for children under 12?
我需要為未滿十二歲以下的孩童買票嗎？

L It depends on the height.
那要看身高。

You need to buy a ticket for children above 115 cm tall.
如果超過一百一十五公分高，那你要幫他買票坐車。

P I see. Can I bring my pet dog into any metro stations?
我了解。請問我可以帶我的寵物狗進站嗎？

L I guess so. I've seen people doing that.
我想是可以的，我有看過人們這樣做。

But you have to put your dog inside a pet box.
但是你要把狗狗裝在寵物箱裡。

關鍵單字

regulation *(n.)*	規定
smoke *(v.)*	抽菸
spite *(v.)*	吐
betel nut *(n. phr.)*	檳榔
juice *(n.)*	汁
chew *(v.)*	嚼
gum *(n.)*	口香糖
litter *(v.)*	亂丟
cigarette *(n.)*	香菸
butts *(n.)*	菸蒂
allow *(v.)*	允許
pet *(n.)*	寵物

• Unit 7

失物招領中心 (1)
The Lost and Found Service Center (Ⅰ)

P: Police officer 警察 F: Finder 拾獲者

F Sir, I just picked up a suitcase in the carriage.
警察先生，我剛在車廂內撿到一只皮箱。

Is there any police office nearby?
這附近有警察局嗎？

Or is it Okay if I just give it to you?
或是我可以直接交給你嗎？

P Just hand it over to Information Desk.
請把物品交給車站詢問處。

They might ask you to fill in a registration form.
他們可能會請您填寫一份表格。

The staff will take over the next procedure and post the message on the bulletin board.
工作人員會承接後續工作，並將訊息公告在佈告欄上。

• Unit 8

失物招領中心 (2)
The Lost and Found Service Center (Ⅱ)

F: Finder 拾獲者　S: Staff 職員

On the phone
電話中

F Hello, this is Debby Cheng.
你好 我是鄭黛比。

Is this the Lost and Found Service Center?
請問這裡是捷運失物招領中心嗎？

S Yes, this is. May I help you?
這裡是，請問有需要為您效勞的地方嗎？

F Sir, I just picked up a suitcase in the Beitou Station.
您好，我剛才在北投車站撿到一只皮箱。

How can I hand it over to the Lost and Found Service Center?
請問我要如何將這只皮箱交到失物招領中心去呢？

S You should take the green line and get off at the Tamsui Station.

你要先搭綠線並在淡水站下車。

Go downstairs to B3 and you will see our office.

走下樓到地下三樓,然後你就會看到我們的辦公室。

F Thank you. I will be there in a minute.

謝謝,我待會兒就到。

關鍵單字

pick up *(v. phr.)*	撿、拾
suitcase *(n.)*	皮箱
carriage *(n.)*	車廂
hand over *(v. phr.)*	繳交
procedure *(n.)*	程序
get off *(v. phr.)*	下(車)
bulletin board *(n. phr.)*	佈告欄

017

Unit 9

票卡資訊
About Ticket Information

P: Passenger 乘客　S: Staff 職員

S May I help you?
有需要效勞的地方嗎？

P I'd like to buy a ticket to the Panchiao Station.
我要買到捷運板橋站的代幣。

S NT$ 45, please.
一共是新台幣四十五元整。

P Can I use this token whenever I like?
我可以在任何時間使用代幣嗎？

S It's valid on the day you buy it.
票券的效期只限購買當日有效。

關鍵單字

token *(n.)*	代幣
afraid *(adj.)*	害怕的
effective *(adj.)*	有效的
same *(adj.)*	相同的
stay *(v.)*	待，停留
overtime *(adv.)*	超過時間

018

• Unit 10

博愛座
About Priority Seats

In the carriage
在車廂內

A child points at a dark blue seat and asks questions of his mother.
一個小孩指著深藍色的座位並問他媽媽問題。

M: Mother 媽媽 S: Son 兒子

S Mom, what are "Priority Seats"?
媽媽，什麼是「博愛座」呢？

M These are seats for people with special needs.
這些座位是給特殊需求者使用的。

S Who are people with special needs?
他們是什麼人？

M They are the elderly, pregnant women, the physically-challenged and little children.
老人家，孕婦，行動不便者及小孩子。

You are a little child.

你是小孩。

You can take a priority seat if no one needs it.

假設沒人要坐，你就可以坐博愛座。

S I see.

這樣我懂了。

M But when you see anyone in need on a train, you should yield your seat to them.

或是你看到那些需要座位的人你應該要讓座給他們。

關鍵單字	
point at *(v. phr.)*	指著
priority *(n.)*	優先權
priority seat *(n. phr.)*	博愛座
pregnant *(n.)*	懷孕的
physically challenged *(adj.)* 身體上有挑戰的，也就是行動不便的	
yield *(v.)*	讓座
train *(n.)*	車廂

019

• Unit 11

微笑單車 (1)
About YouBikes（Ⅰ）

Janet comes from the U.K.
珍奈特來自英國。

She and David take the MRT to the
Taipei City Hall Station.
她跟大衛搭捷運到了台北市政府站。

J: Janet 珍奈特 D: David 大衛

J Wow, what are those bright bikes?
哇，這些亮色的腳踏車是什麼？

D They are YouBikes.
這是微笑單車 YouBikes。

J What are they?
那是什麼？

D YouBike is actually a public transport subsystem.
微笑單車 YouBikes 實際上是公眾運輸系統。

In 2009, Taipei City's Department of Transportation introduced this bicycle rental program to facilitate the transportation in the city.

台北市政府交通局在2009年推出這種單車租借計畫來促進城市裡的交通狀況。

J That's cool! Can I use one of them?
聽起來真酷！我可以用嗎？

D Sure. All you need is an EasyCard!
當然啊，你所需要的就是一張悠遊卡！

J Great! I have one.
太好了，我有一張。

關鍵單字

bright *(adj.)*	明亮的，亮色的
hall *(n.)*	廳堂
public transport *(n. phr.)*	公眾運輸
facilitate *(v.)*	促進

020

• Unit 12

微笑單車 (2)
About YouBikes (Ⅱ)

David takes Janet to a YouBike rental station kiosk and teaches her how to rent a YouBike.

大衛帶珍奈特到微笑單車租借亭，並教她如何租微笑單車。

J: Janet 珍奈特 D: David 大衛

D First, you have to register as a YouBike member at the rental station kiosk or register on YouBike's official website.

首先，你要在微笑單車租借亭註冊微笑單車會員，或是上微笑單車官方網站註冊。

J Well, let's get registered!

好喔，我們就來註冊吧！

After a while.

過了一陣子

J Now, I am a registered member.

現在我是註冊會員了。

Can I use one of these cute bikes now?
現在我可以用這些可愛的腳踏車了嗎？

D Well, now you can select a bicycle you like.
嗯，現在你可以挑一台你喜歡的腳踏車。

Put your Easy Card on the sensor pad
and pick up your bicycle at the selected
parking pole within 90 seconds.
把你的悠遊卡放在感應區，然後90秒內將車
從停車柱拿出來。

J Yes! I get it. I can cycle about the city at last!
太好了，我弄好了。我終於可以騎腳踏車繞
台北市了！

D The good news is that the first 30 minutes
of your ride is free!
好消息是前三十分鐘免費！

After that, you have to pay at NT$ 10 per
30 minutes by your EasyCard.
三十分鐘之後，你要用悠遊卡支付每30分鐘
10元台幣。

J OK. OK. Let's go!
好啦，好啦。我們走吧！

D Don't forget to return the bike at the kiosk.
別忘了到租借亭還車喔。

kiosk *(n.)*	亭子
register *(v.)*	註冊
sensor *(n.)*	感應器
member *(n.)*	成員，會員

Part 4

台灣高鐵

Taiwan High Speed Rail

Taipei is so fun!

時刻表
About the Timetable

Mary comes from Canada.
瑪莉來自加拿大。

She will visit her friends in Kaohsiung by Taiwan High Speed Rail (THSR) from Taoyuan.
她打算要搭乘高鐵去拜訪在高雄的朋友。

On the phone
電話中

M: Mary 瑪莉 F: Friend 朋友

Ⓜ Hi, can you help me book a THSR ticket to Kaohsiung?
嗨，你能幫我訂一張往高雄的高鐵車票嗎？

I have no idea about the transportation system in Taiwan.
我對台灣交通系統不熟。

F Sure.
可以。

Have you decided when you are leaving?
決定何時要出發了嗎？

M I am not sure. Can I find a timetable on the website?
我不確定。網站上有時刻表嗎？

F Yeah, I think you can go to the THSR website.
嗯，我想你可以看看高鐵的網站。

You can select English on the top of your right hand side.
右上角可以選擇英語翻譯。

On the website, you can use its timetable, fare finder,
你可以在網頁使用時刻及票價查訊系統。

or its online booking system.
或線上訂位系統。

This THSR's website is very user- friendly.

高鐵的網站非常人性化。

I am sure you will not have any problems with it.

我相信你一定不會有問題。

Ⓜ Thank you.

謝謝你。

Ⓕ You are welcome.

不用客氣啦。

關鍵單字

transportation *(n.)*	交通
system *(n.)*	系統
timetable *(n.)*	時刻表
website *(n.)*	網站
fare *(n.)*	票價

• Unit 2

線上訂票系統
About the Online Booking System

Mary is going to book a THSR ticket.
瑪莉正要訂高鐵票。

On the phone
電話中

M: Mary 瑪莉　C: Customer Service 客戶服務

C Hello, it's Taiwan High Speed Rail. How may I help you?
您好，這裡是台灣高鐵。請問有需要服務的地方嗎？

M Hello, This is Mary Watson from Canada.
我是來自加拿大的凱瑪莉。

I have some problems booking THSR tickets on line.
我在網路訂高鐵票時遇到些問題。

C Yes, Miss Watson. May I ask what kind of problem it is?
好的，華生小姐。請問您遇到的問題是什麼呢？

M I'm wondering if a foreigner can book a THSR ticket?

我想知道外國人也可以訂票嗎？

C Of course. You can use the online booking system on our website.

當然可以。你可以利用我們的網站上的線上訂票系統。

We have "English" version of our website.

你可以選擇英文版本。

On the top of the right you will find "English" to click.

在右上角的地方你可以找到英文選項。

Then choose Ticketing Information on the top, and you'll find Online Booking.

然後選擇票務資訊，你就能找到線上訂位系統。

M I see. Thank you very much. I have one more question.

明白了，非常謝謝你。我還有一個問題。

C Yes, please.

好的，請說。

M My flight will arrive in Taipei.

我的飛機抵達的目的地是台北。

But the name of the airport is Taiwan Taoyuan International Airport.
但是機場名稱卻是桃園國際機場。

I'm not sure which THSR station I should select.
我不確定我應該要選哪一個高鐵車站。

C Taoyuan station. You can take Bus 705 from Airport to Taoyuan THSR station.
桃園站。機場到高鐵桃園站,可以搭乘 705 號公車。

M OK. I just confirm the trip details.
好的。我剛剛確認了訂位明細,

But your website asks me to fill in contact person information.
但是網站要求我要填寫聯絡人資料。

Does the contact person have to be a Taiwanese?
聯絡人一定要是台灣人嗎?

C No, you can just fill in your personal information.
不用，您可以填入您的個人資料即可。

Then, you need to agree with the regulations
然後，你必須同意相關規定，

and confirm the booking order on the website.
並確認網路訂單。

You can choose how to pay the ticket fare.
你可以在我們網路上選擇你付費的方式。

M I got it.
了解。

C Is there any further question, Ms. Watson?
不用客氣。還有其他的疑問嗎？

M No. That's all. Thank you very much!
沒有問題了。非常感謝您！

C You are welcome. It's our honor to be able to help you.

不用客氣。能為您服務是我們的榮幸。

Thank you for calling us and wish you have a nice day.

感謝您撥打電話。祝您有美好的一天。

關鍵單字

book *(v.)*	訂票
version *(n.)*	版本
confirm *(v.)*	確認
order *(n.)*	訂單

• Unit 3

退票處理
Asking for Refunds

M: Mary Watson 瑪莉
C: Customer Service 客戶服務

C Thank you for calling THSR Customer Service.
感謝您的來電這邊是高鐵客服部。

This is Lin Speaking.
我是林。

How can I help you?
有需要幫忙的地方嗎？

M I booked a ticket online. But now I have to cancel my ticket.
我在網路上訂了票，但我現在必須要取消訂票。

C May I have you name, please?
請問該如何稱呼呢？

M Mary, Mary Watson.
瑪莉，瑪莉華生。

C Ms. Watson. I need to check your identification number first.
華生小姐，我需要先確認您的認證號碼。

Your reservation number or passport number, please.
你登記的號碼或護照號碼？

M My passport number is 1234567 and the reservation number is 99887766.
我的護照號碼是 1234567，而登記號碼是 99887766。

C A moment, please. The system is going to search for your ticket information.
請等一下，系統將查詢您的票務資訊。

Your ticket is from the Taoyuan Station to the Zuoying Station.
你訂的車票是從桃園站到左營站。

A surcharge of 20 dollars per ticket will be charged for ticket refund.
申請退票，每張車票將會索取20元手續費。

Are you certain that you want to cancel this booking order, Ms. Watson?
華生小姐，您確定要取消這次訂位了嗎？

M Yes, please.
是的，麻煩您。

C OK. Your booking order has been cancelled.
好的，您的訂位紀錄已被取消。

Is there anything else I can help you?
還有什麼需要我幫忙的地方嗎？

M No. Thank you very much.
了解了。謝謝您。

C You are welcome. Wish you have a great day. Good bye.
不用客氣。祝您有美好的一天。再會。

關鍵單字

cancel *(v.)*	取消
identification *(n.)*	身分
reservation *(n.)*	登記
refund *(n.)*	退票
surcharge *(n.)*	處理費
certain *(adj.)*	確定的

• Unit 4

廣播服務 (1)
About Announcements (I)

T. C: Train Controller 廣播員

T.C Ladies and Gentlemen, attention, please.
各位旅客請注意。

The train number 123 bound for Taipei
is now approaching the A side platform.
要前往台北123的車次即將進到A側月台邊。

It will depart after five minutes.
五分鐘後準備發車。

Please mind the platform gap when you
board the train.
當你上車時，請留意月台邊間隙。

We wish you a pleasant journey.
祝你有美好的旅程。

Thank you for your cooperation.
謝謝你的合作。

controller *(n.)*	管理員
gentleman *(n.)*	紳士
attention *(n.)*	注意
be bound for *(v. phr.)*	前往
approach *(v.)*	靠近
gap *(n.)*	間隙
pleasant *(adj.)*	美好的
journey *(n.)*	旅程
cooperation *(n.)*	合作

025

• Unit 5

廣播服務 (2)
About Announcements (Ⅱ)

T. C: Train Controller 廣播員

T.C Dear Guests.
親愛的來賓您好。

We are looking for a boy in a blue sportswear and a pair of white shoes.
我們在尋找一位穿藍色運動服與白色球鞋的男孩。

He is about 130 centimeters tall.
他大約身高130公分高。

If you see him, please take him to the information desk.
如果您見到此男孩,請他到服務櫃檯來。

Or contact us as soon as you hear our broadcasting.
或是當你聽到廣播,請馬上與我們連繫。

Your family is waiting for you.
您的家人在等您。

Thank you for your help.

感謝您的協助。

關鍵單字

look for *(v. phr.)*	尋找	
sportswear *(n.)*	運動服	
contact *(v.)*	聯絡	
broadcast *(n.)*	廣播	

026

• Unit 6

遺失服務中心
About the Lost and Found Service Center

M: Mary 瑪莉　A: Agent 代理處

A Is this the lost and found service center?
這裡是失物招領處嗎??

A Yes, how can I help you?
是的,有哪裡需要幫忙嗎?

M I left my purse on the train.
我把皮包留在列車上了。

A When did you notice that?
請問您何時注意到這件事的呢?

M I found it lost when I got off at Zuoying Station around three o'clock.
我是大約在下午三點左營站下車時發現的。

The train number was 1234.

車次是編號1234。

A Can you describe the features of your lost purse?

能描述一下你那個遺失皮包的特徵嗎？

M It's a brown leather purse.

咖啡色皮包。

And it is old and small.

而且它很舊又小。

A Okay. Would you please fill out this form?

好的，麻煩你填寫一下這份表單。

M Sure. How long do you think it would take to find my purse?

沒問題。你認為包包需要多久時間找到？

A It depends.
看狀況而定。

We couldn't guarantee anything at this point.
我們不能保證任何事情。

But we will try our best to look for it.
但我們會盡力找尋。

關鍵單字

leave *(v.)*	遺留
purse *(n.)*	女用皮包
notice *(v.)*	注意到
describe *(v.)*	描述
brown *(adj.)*	咖啡色
leather *(n.)*	皮革
guarantee *(v.)*	保證

• Unit 7

乘車指南
Asking for Information Pamphlets

M: Mary 瑪莉　F: Friend 朋友

M Hello, are there any information pamphlets for passengers?
嗨，請問那邊有給乘客的資訊手冊呢？

F Yes, you can see that we have many kinds of pamphlets,
有的，我們各種資訊手冊，

like station information, the station facilities, the safety needs and the regulation.
像是車站資訊、車站設施、安全須知及相關規定。

Which one do you want?
你要哪種？

M I am not sure.
我還不清楚。

But I am wondering whether I can carry the luggage with us on the train?
但是我想知道我可以帶行李上車廂嗎？

F Yes, you can bring your luggage onto the train,
你可以帶行李上車廂，

except dangerous goods, like bombs, firework,
但是危險的物品像是炸彈、煙火

or any goods that contain inflammable material.
以及任何含有易燃性的物品就不可以。

If you have any further questions,
假如你有任何問題，

you can call the customer service or ask our staff.
你可以打客服專線或是問我們的職員。

They are happy to answer your questions about how to use the facilities in a carriage.
他們樂意回答您如何使用相關設施。

關鍵單字

pamphlet *(n.)*	手冊
safety *(n.)*	安全
luggage *(n.)*	行李
carry *(v.)*	攜帶
except *(prep.)*	除了…之外
dangerous *(adj.)*	危險的
bomb *(n.)*	炸彈
firework *(n.)*	煙火
goods *(n. pl.)*	貨品，物品
contain *(v.)*	包含
inflammable *(adj.)*	易燃的
material *(n.)*	物質

• Unit 8

設施服務

Asking about Facilities on a Train

M: Mary 瑪莉 S: Staff 職員

M Excuse me, is there a vending machine on the train?
請問在車廂內有自動販賣機嗎？

S Yes, you can find one on the 1st, the 5th and the 11th carriage.
有的，你可以在第一節車廂，第五節車廂，及第十一節車廂找到自動販賣機。

M How many carriages do you have in the train?
請問一組列車有多少車廂呢？

S We have twelve carriages.
一般來說，目前是一組列車有十二節車廂。

The 6th train is a business carriage.
從第六節是商務車廂。

Some carriages have disabled seats with the toilet for our service.
有些車廂附設無障礙座位及洗手間服務。

vending machine *(n. phr.)*	自動販賣機
carriage *(n.)*	車廂
business carriage *(n. phr.)*	商務車廂
disabled seat *(n. phr.)*	無障礙座位
toilet *(n.)*	洗手間，馬桶

•Unit 9

取票服務
Asking for Ticket Collection

On the phone
電話中

M: Mary 瑪莉　F: Friend 朋友

M Hi, I booked a ticket on THRS website. I'm so looking forward to seeing you!
嗨，我在高鐵網站訂好車票了。好期待跟你見面呢！

F Wow, that's great! I can't wait!
哇！真是太棒了! 我等不及了！

M But I have a question.
但我有個問題耶。

Do you know where I can get the ticket I reserved online?
你知道我要去哪裡才得到在網路上訂的車票呢？

F You can get tickets from any convenience stores in Taiwan.
現在你都可在台灣任一家便利商店內取票。

M That is so convenient!
真是太方便了！

F But you have to pay for the handling fee when you get your ticket in a convenience store.
但是你在便利商店取票時還是得付手續費。

M How much is the handling fee?
手續費要多少錢呢？

F It will cost you 13 dollars.
台幣十三元。

M I got it. But can't I just collect the ticket in the THSR station?
我了解了。但是, 我不能直接在高鐵車站取票嗎？

F Yeah, sure!
當然可以啊！

關鍵單字		
look forward to *(v. phr.)*	期待
reserve *(v.)*	預訂
collect the ticket *(v. phr.)*	取票

• Unit 10

促銷專案
Looking for Discounts

M: Mary 瑪莉 S: Staff 職員

Ⓜ Excuse me. I've heard that there is a discount for those who book THSR tickets early.
抱歉，我最近聽說早些訂高鐵會有折扣。

Is that true?
這是真的嗎？

Ⓢ Yes, you can get some discounts for early bird tickets.
有的，早鳥票有些折扣。

You will get 35 percent to 10 percent off.
大概是折百分之三十五到百分之十。

Ⓜ It sounds good. Do you have any other ticket with discounts?
聽起來還不錯。你們還有其他種車票有優惠的嗎？

Ⓢ Yes, we also provide peuodic tickets with 21% discount.
有的，我們還有提供79折的回數票優惠。

It allows you to take non-reserved seats for 8 times in 45 days.

可以在四十五天內搭乘自由座8次。

M It may not be suitable for me. Do you offer group tickets?

這個可能不太適合我。你們有賣團體票嗎？

S Yes, we have. For a group more than 11 people can have 5% discount.

有的，十一人以上訂票，可享有 95 折的優惠。

Same itinerary and same departure time are both required.

出發地點、時間，以及目的地必須相同。

We also work with some businesses and offer their staff ticket packages.

我們也有跟某些企業合作，提供套票。

M Cool! I am going to tell my friend. Thank you!

酷喔！我要去通知親友。感謝您！

關鍵單字

percent *(n.)*	百分比
peroidic *(adj.)*	定期的
peroidic ticket *(n. phr.)*	回數票
allow *(v.)*	允許
suitable *(adj.)*	適合的
offer *(v.)*	提供
itinerary *(n.)*	行程
departure *(n.)*	出發
require *(v.)*	要求
work with *(v. phr.)*	與…合作
business *(n.)*	產業，生意
staff *(n.)*	全體職員
package ticket *(n. phr.)*	套票
inform *(v.)*	通知

Part

5

公車

Buses in Taipei

Taipei is so fun!

•Unit 1

乘坐公車
Take a Bus

Chris is asking a passer-by how to get to the Tianmu Baseball Stadium by bus.

奎斯詢問路人要如何坐公車到天母棒球場。

C: Chris 奎斯 P: Passer-by 路人
B: Bus driver 公車司機

C Does this bus go to the Tianmu Baseball Stadium?

這班公車有到天母棒球場嗎？

B No, this bus does not go to the Tianmu Baseball Stadium.

這班車沒到天母棒球場。

C Which bus should I take to get there?

那要搭幾號公車才能到那裏呢？

B You should take Bus 206.

你應該搭 206 號。

C Where is the bus stop?

我要在哪邊等車呢?

P Right there. At that stop.

就在那裏,那個站牌。

C Do you happen to know how often Bus 206 comes?

你知道206號公車多久來一班嗎?

P About every fifteen minutes.

大約十五分鐘來一班。

C Is it rush hour now?

請問現在是尖峰時間嗎?

P Yes, it is. It may be very crowded.

是的,現在可能會很擁擠。

C Thanks for your help.

謝謝你的幫忙。

關鍵單字

passer-by *(n.)*	路人
Tianmu Baseball Stadium *(n.)*	
	天母棒球場
stop *(n.)*	站牌
bus stop *(n. phr.)*	公車站牌
come by *(v. phr.)*	從旁走過
rush *(adj.)*	匆忙的
rush hour *(n. phr.)*	交通尖峰時刻
crowded *(adj.)*	擁擠的

032

• Unit 2

電子公車站牌
About Electronic Bus Stops

There are new electronic bus stops in the streets.

街頭上出現了電子公車站牌。

C: Chris 奎斯　Tina 緹娜　P: Passer-by 路人

T Wow, Look!

喔，看啊！

That's the new LED display system.

這是新的 LED 顯示系統。

C What is that？

那是什麼東西呢？

T This is a new bus bulletin board system.

那是新的公車電子佈告欄。

P Yes, and it can display the arrival time of each bus.

沒錯。而且它可以顯示每輛公司到達時間。

C How does the system work?
那是怎麼顯示出來的呢？

P By the global positioning system of the buses.
透過公車上的 GPS 定位。

C How long does it take to get to the Tianmu Baseball Stadium?
要多久才能到天母棒球場呢？

T The bus bulletin board system says it will take five minutes.
我看公車電子佈告欄說要 5 分鐘。

Here comes the bus!
公車來了！

C Hurry up. We will get on Bus 206.
趕快。我們要搭乘 206 公車了。

關鍵單字

bulletin board *(n. phr.)*	佈告欄	
electronic *(adj.)*	電子的	
global positioning system (GPS) *(n. phr.)*		
	衛星定位	

033

• Unit 3

在台北過馬路
Crossing a Street in Taipei

C: Chris 奎斯 P: Passer-by 路人

C Excuse me. I'm looking for a supermarket.
對不起，我在找超市。

Is there one nearby?
請問這邊附近有嗎？

P Just cross the street, and you will find it.
過馬路你就會看到了。

But for your safety, you can use the pedestrian bridge.
但為了安全起見，你可以走陸橋。

C Why?
為什麼呢？

P Many scooters and cars travel at a high speed.
有許多機車及汽車都高速行駛。

This causes accidents in the intersection.

常在會在十字路口發生事故。

C Well, thanks a lot.

好吧，多謝了。

關鍵單字

supermarket *(n.)*	超市
pedestrian bridge *(n. phr.)*	陸橋
traffic *(n.)*	交通
speed *(n.)*	速度
accident *(n.)*	事故
intersection *(n.)*	十字路口

034

Unit 4

注意號誌
About the Traffic Lights

Tina is ready to go through the traffic light.
緹娜正準備要過紅綠燈。

C: Chris 奎斯 Tina 緹娜

C Hi! Tina, Hurry up.
嗨！緹娜，走快一點。

The little green man is walking.
小綠人在開始走路。

T The traffic signal is quite special.
是滿特別的交通號誌。

Isn't it strange to see the green light flashing?
綠燈正在閃光是不是有點奇怪呢？

C It means that pedestrains who want to cross the road need to hurry up!
那表示想要過馬路的行人要加快腳步了。

The traffic signal is showing the seconds for pedestrians to cross the road.

那是交通號誌顯示行人過路的秒數。

When you walk in the streets and are about to go through the traffic light,

當你站在街上正要過紅綠燈時,

pay attention to your steps and wait for the green light.

請注意你的腳步及注意到綠燈號誌。

Whenever you see a red light, you have to stop and stay by the road.

每當你看到紅燈,你就要停下來待在路邊。

C These are useful facilities for pedestrians in Taiwan.

這是對於台灣行人便利的交通設施。

關鍵單字	
traffic light *(n. phr.)*	紅綠燈
traffic signal *(n. phr.)*	交通號誌
strange *(adj.)*	奇怪的
shine *(v.)*	發光
signal *(n.)*	號誌

035

Part

6

租車服務

Car Rental Service

Taipei is
so fun!

• Unit 1

如何租車 (1)
Car Rental (I)

C: Chris 奎斯 L: Leaser 租賃業者

C Hi, I'd like to rent a car for six days.
我想要租車六天

L May I see your driver's license, please?
我可以先看你的駕照嗎？

C Here's my international driver's license.
這是我的國際駕照。

How many drivers do you have?
請問有幾位駕駛者呢？

C Only one.
只有一位。

L Just fill out this form.
請填寫這張表格。

Write down your address here and sign your name on the bottom of the page.
將你的地址寫在這裡，並在文件底下簽名。

By the way, the collision insurance is included.
順道告知這次租車內含碰撞險。

C Do I need to purchase other insurance?
那我還有需要買其他保險嗎？

L It depends on your needs.
看你的需要。

關鍵單字	
rent *(v.)*	租
license *(n.)*	許可證
international *(adj.)*	國際的
international driver's license. *(n. phr.)*	
	國際駕照
sign *(v.)*	簽名
collision *(n.)*	碰撞
insurance *(n.)*	保險
depend on *(v. phr.)*	依照；取決於

• Unit 2

如何租車 (2)
Car Rental (Ⅱ)

C: Chris 奎斯 L: Leaser 租賃業者

C I am wondering how to return the car?
我想請教如何還車。

If I rent a car in Hsinchu City, do I have to return it to the same location?
如果我在新竹市租車,我是否需要在相同地點還車嗎?

L No, you can drop it off at any our local branches.
不用,你可以把車還在本地的分公司。

C That's great.
太棒了。

Is there anything else that I should pay attention to?
還有其他要注意的地方嗎?

L Our daily driving range limit is four hundred kilometers.
每日限駛里程數四百公里。

If you are late to return the car, we will charge you the additional fee.
如果你還車時間遲了，我們會加收額外的費用。

C How much is it to rent this car?
租這部車要多少錢呢？

L It costs NT $12,800.
要一萬兩千八百元整。

C Okay, I will take it.
好的，我要租這台車。

Where is the car key?
車鑰匙是在哪裡呢？

L Here you are.
在這裡。

C Should I fill up the gas tank?
我應該要加滿油嗎？

L Yes. You should fill it up to hit the road.
沒錯。你需要加滿油才能上路。

Our cars use the unleaded gasoline.
我們的車都使用無鉛汽油。

C I get it.
我知道了。

關鍵單字

drop off *(v. phr.)*	下車
local *(adj.)*	本地的
branch *(n.)*	分公司
kilometer *(n.)*	公里
additional *(adj.)*	附加的
consider *(v.)*	視為
damage *(n.)*	損害
fill up *(v. phr.)*	裝滿
gas tank *(n. phr.)*	油槽

037

•Unit 3

找尋停車位
Look for a Parking Lot

C: Chris 奎斯 T: Tina 緹娜 P: Passer-by 路人

T Is there a parking lot near the theater?
劇院附近有停車場嗎?

C I am not sure. I will ask someone.
不確定。我會再問路人。

I think we can find a car space.
我想應該會找到停車位。

Ten minutes later 十分鐘後。

C Excuse me. What is the street?
請問這是哪一條街呢?

I am looking for Emei Car Park.
我要到峨嵋街停車場。

Do you know how to get there?

你知道要怎麼去嗎？

P Well, let me see. Go straight for two blocks, and then turn right.

那我想想看。往那裏走經過兩條街，然後向右轉。

It's just around the corner.

它就是在轉角的地方。

C OK. Thank you very much.

好。非常感謝。

關鍵單字

parking lot *(n. phr.)*	停車場
parking space *(n. phr.)*	停車位
car park *(n. phr.)*	停車場
theater *(n.)*	戲院
block *(n.)*	街區
turn right *(v. phr.)*	向右轉
corner *(n.)*	轉角

038

· Unit 4

繳費規定
Payment Regulations

Chris is entering the car park and prepares to park his car.

奎斯進入停車場準備要停車了。

C: Chris 奎斯 G: Guard 警衛

C How much does it cost to park a car?

停車要多少錢呢？

G We charge you 30 dollars per hour in the weekdays, 50 dollars per hour on weekends and on holidays.

平日一小時30元整, 例假日或是周末則是一小時50元整。

We are not responsible for your valuables.

我們不負保管責任。

So, please park your vehicle well and lock your windows and doors.

所以，請把你的車停妥，並鎖好車窗與車門。

Take the valuables with you when leaving the car park.

並將貴重物品帶離停車場。

Here is your parking token.

這是你的停車枚。

C How do I pay the car parking fee?

要怎麼付停車費呢？

G You should insert the token to the payment machine.

你要先到繳費機投遞停車枚。

Then, you'll see your car parking fee on the screen.

然後，你會在螢幕上看到你的停車金額。

You can pay by credit card or cash.

可以用信用卡也可以用現金付帳。

That's all.

就這樣子。

C I get it.

那我了解。

關鍵單字

weekdays *(n. pl.)*	平日
weekend *(n.)*	周末
holiday *(n.)*	假日
vehicle *(n.)*	車輛
lock *(v.)*	上鎖
valuables *(n. pl.)*	貴重物品
car parking fee *(n. phr)*	停車費
car parking token *(n. phr.)*	停車枚
payment machine *(n.phr.)*	繳費機

Chapter 2

住宿

Accommodations 039

PAPAGO

飯店訂房

Hotel Reservation

Taipei is so fun!

• Unit 1

網路預約 (1)

Making a Room Reservation Online (Ⅰ)

Hulk is an exchange student from the U. K. Freya is his host mother in Taiwan.
浩克是從英國來的交換學生。芙蕾雅是他的寄宿家庭母親。

Now, Hulk seems to search for something on the internet.
現在浩克好像在網路上尋找什麼東西。

H: Hulk 浩克　F: Freya 芙蕾雅

F Good morning! What are you doing in such an early morning?
早安，你一大早在作什麼？

H Good morning, I want to book a room at the Grand Hotel online.
早安, 我想要用網路預訂圓山大飯店的房間。

But I don't know how to do that.
但是我不知道要怎麼弄。

F You can make the online reservation through their booking system.
你可經由訂房系統先進行線上預約。

H Is it safe?
這樣安全嗎？

F Yes. It's secure, free, fast and easy.
安全。而且免費、快速、操作簡便。

H How do I use its booking system?
我要如何操作使用預約系統呢？

F You just choose the date, number of persons, the type of room and number of beds in each room for each night.
選擇你要入住日期、每晚每間人數、房型、床數等需求。

They will also need your credit card information as guarantee.
另外也需要您的信用卡資料作為擔保。

H Do they accept any credit cards?
他們接受任何一家的信用卡嗎？

F Some might not accept VISA electron or Maestro cards for online reservations.
在網路預約上，有些不接受電子式的 Visa 或 Maestro 信用卡。

• Unit 2

網路預約 (2)
Making a Room Reservation Online (Ⅱ)

Freya is teaching Hulk how to reserve a hotel room online.

芙蕾雅正在教浩克如何網路預訂飯店房間。

H: Hulk 浩克　F: Freya 芙蕾雅

H Well, how about the cancellation policy?

嗯，那取消訂房的規定呢？

F It depends.

每一家不一樣。

Some might charge you if you don't cancel the booking two days before your arrival day.

有些會要求你在入住日期兩天前取消，否則要收取費用。

If the cancellation is late, some would fully charge you for the first night.

有些會因為晚於事前取消預約時間，而收取第一晚的全額費用。

H Could I make a reservation by email?
我可以先用電子郵件作預約嗎?

F Yes, some also accept the order by email.
可以，有些也接受郵件訂單。

And they would send you a confirmation
letter with instructions on how to
securely send your credit card numbers
and expire date.
而且會發送指示確認信，告知如何安全地提
供信用卡號碼及有效日期。

H How do I get the receipt of payment?
我要如何取得付款收據呢？

F It will be made after your payment during
your stay.
你付款入住後就可以拿到入住收據。

H Do I have to pay a deposit in advance?
有需要事先預付訂金嗎？

F Yes, some regulations require you to pay
the half amount to the specific account.
是的，有些規定是須支付一半訂金到指定帳
戶。

H Wow! You know a lot! Thank you.
哇！你知道的真多！謝謝你。

關鍵單字

cancellation *(n.)*	取消
confirmation *(n.)*	確認
instruction *(n.)*	指示
securely *(adv.)*	安全地
expire date *(n. phr.)*	有效日期
payment *(n.)*	付款
regulation *(n.)*	規定
require *(v.)*	要求
specific *(adj.)*	特定的

Unit 3

電話預約 (1)

Making a Room Reservation by Phone (Ⅰ)

Amy is salesperson living in Japan.
艾咪是一位住在日本的業務人員。

She is going to Taiwan tomorrow for a business trip.
她明天要到台灣出差。

Now, she is booking a hotel room on the phone.
現在她正在電話上預訂飯店房間。

A: Amy 艾咪　F. R.: Front Reception 櫃台部

F.R. Smile Hotel. May I help you？
　　微笑飯店您好，有需要服務地方嗎？

A Yes. I urgently need a room for tomorrow night.
　　有的，我現在急需明晚要入住的房間。

Do you have any vacancies?
請問還有空房嗎？

F.R. Yes, we have. What sort of room would you like?

有的，請問您想要哪一種房型？

A I would like a suite, please.

我要一間套房。

F.R.: Just a moment, please. Yes, we have one, madam.

請等一下。有的，女士，我們有一間。

A What is the price of the suite for one night?

請問房價一晚多少？

F.R. It is NT $8,400 per night.

一晚是新台幣八千四百元整。

A That's a bit more than I expected.

這比我想像要貴。

Could you give me a discount?

你能給我一些折扣嗎？

F.R. No, I am afraid not, sorry.

恐怕是沒有的。非常抱歉。

A It is a pity. Do you have a less expensive suite?

真是可惜。請問有便宜一點的套房嗎?

F.R. Well, it is the least expensive suite for tomorrow night.

嗯,這是到明晚最便宜的套房了。

A OK, I will take it.

只好這樣了。

關鍵單字

salesperson *(n.)*	業務
business trip *(n. phr.)*	商旅,出差
urgently *(adv.)*	急迫地
vacancy *(n.)*	空房
suite *(n.)*	套房

• Unit 4

電話預約 (2)

Making a Room Reservation by Phone (Ⅱ)

Amy is reserving a hotel room on the phone.

Amy 正在電話中預約飯店房間。

A: Amy 艾咪 F. R.: Front Reception 櫃台部

A Is breakfast included in the price?
請問房間價錢有含早餐嗎？

F.R. Yes, it is included, madam.
有的，女士。

May I have your name, please?
請問您尊姓大名？

A Amy. Amy Wang.
艾咪。王艾咪。

F.R. And your phone number, please.
請問您的電話號碼？

A 0966-588699。

0966-588699。

F.R. Thank you, Ms. Wang. One suite tomorrow.

謝謝您，王小姐。預訂明晚套房一間。

How many nights do you expect to stay?

請問您預計入住幾晚上呢？

A About three nights.

大約三個晚上。

F.R. OK. One suite for three nights has been reserved for you, Ms. Wang.

好的，已為您預定好一間套房三個晚上。

You may check in after three p.m.

您三點後就可以辦理入住。

A OK. Thank you!

好的，謝謝！

F.R. You are welcome. And we sincerely look forward to your visit.

請不用客氣。我們誠心地期待您的到訪。

• Unit 5

入住登記 (1)
Hotel Check-in (I)

Amy is salesperson from Japan.
艾咪是一位來自日本的業務人員。

She comes to Taiwan for a business trip.
她來台灣出差。

Now, she arrives at the hotel.
現在她到飯店了。

A: Amy 艾咪 F.R.: Front Reception 櫃台部

F.R. Good morning, madam. Welcome to the Smile Hotel.
早安，女士，歡迎光臨微笑飯店。

May I help you?
我能為您效勞嗎？

A Yes, I have a reservation.
我在這邊有預約。

F.R. May I have your name, please?
請問尊姓大名？

A Amy Wang. A-M-Y, W-A-N-G.
王艾咪。A-M-Y, W-A-N-G.

F.R. How long do you expect to stay?
請問您預計要待多久呢？

A Three nights.
三晚左右。

F.R. Yes, madam. We have a suite for you, reserved for 3 nights.
小姐您好，我們替你保留了一間套房，預訂三個晚上。

Do you have a passport with you?
請問有帶護照嗎？我需要查看。

A Sure. Here it is.
有的，在這裡。

F.R. Great. Would you please fill out this form for me?
好的，可以麻煩您填寫登記表嗎？

Ⓐ Okay. Do I have to sign here?
好的。我需要在這簽名嗎?

F.R. Yes, please. How would you like to pay?
是的,麻煩您。請問要如何付款?

Ⓐ By credit card.
用信用卡付款。

Which credit card do you accept?
請問這裡能接受哪家信用卡?

F.R. Any one will do.
任何一間都可以。

Ⓐ Here you are.
這是我的卡。

關鍵單字

check-in *(n. phr.)*	入房登記
expect *(v.)*	預計

• Unit 6

入住登記 (2)
Hotel Check-in (Ⅱ)

Amy is checking in at Smile Hotel. She has just paid her room by credit card.

Amy正在微笑飯店入住登記。她剛用信用卡付完房錢。

A: Amy 艾咪　F.R.: Front Reception 櫃台部

F.R. Sorry to keep you waiting.

抱歉讓你久等。

Ms. Wang, here are your passport, a room key and breakfast vouchers.

王小姐，這是您的護照，客房鑰匙和早餐券。

Your room number is 601 on the 6th floor.

您的房間在六樓，601號房。

The bellboy will take your bags and show you to your room.

門房員會替您提行李並帶您到房間。

Wish you enjoy your stay with us.

希望您在我們這邊住得愉快。

A What time does breakfast service finish?
請問早餐供應到幾點呢？

F.R. Our breakfast service starts at 7 a.m. and ends at 10 a.m..
早餐供應時間是從早上七點到十點左右。

The dining hall is on the 2nd floor.
餐廳在本棟的二樓。

A Thank you. Do you have any room services?
謝謝。這邊有提供客房服務嗎？

F.R. We provide meal delivery and laundry service.
我們有提供飲食及送洗服務。

A Do you have hotel facilities?
這邊有飯店設施可以讓房客使用嗎？

F.R. Yes, we have indoor/outdoor swimming pool, a sauna, a gymnasium and two beauty salons.
我們有室內外泳池，桑拿浴，健身房和兩間美容院。

A I got it.
我知道了。

關鍵單字

voucher *(n.)*	收據
bellboy *(n.)*	服務生
room service *(n. phr.)*	客房服務
delivery *(n.)*	遞送
laundry *(n.)*	洗衣
sauna *(n.)*	桑拿浴
gymnasium *(n.)*	健身房
beauty salon *(n. phr.)*	美容院

045

• Unit 7

客房服務 (1)
Rome Service（Ⅰ）

Hulk is an exchange student from the U. K.
浩克是來自英國的交換學生。

He is now living at Smile Hotel and asking for room service on the phone.
浩克正下榻於微笑飯店，正在電話中要求客房服務。

H: Hulk 浩克 R: Room Service 客房服務

Ⓡ Good evening, Sir. This is Room Service.
晚安，先生。這邊是客房服務。

What can I do for you?
請問你需要什麼服務呢？

Ⓗ Hi. This is room 802.
你好，這裡是802號房。

I'd like a wake-up call at 7:00 tomorrow, please.
我要明天早上七點的晨喚服務。

Ⓡ Okay, You'll get a wake-up call at 7:00 from our automated service tomorrow.

好的。您將會接到我們自動電話的晨喚服務，時間訂在明天早上七點。

wake-up call *(n. phr.)*　　電話晨喚服務

• Unit 8

客房服務 (2)
Room Service (Ⅱ)

Hulk is asking for the room service on the phone.

浩克正在電話中要求客房服務。

H: Hulk 浩克 R: Room Service 客房服務

R Do you need anything else?

還有其他的需求嗎？

H Yes, I want to order some food. What kind of food do you have?

我還需要點餐。請問你們供應什麼呢？

R We serve basic meals.

我們有提供基本餐點。

There's a menu on the table.

桌上有菜單。

You may take a look.

您可參考看看。

H I see. I want one order of fried egg with bacon, a pot of coffee, a Caesar salad and two orders of toasts.

看到了。我要一份培根加煎蛋，一壺咖啡，一份凱薩沙拉和二份吐司。

R Any desserts?

需要甜點嗎？

H No, that's all. Thanks.

不用，這樣就好，謝謝你。

R Sure. Let me repeat your order.

好的，讓我重複一下您的餐點。

One set of fried egg with bacon, a pot of coffee, a Caesar salad and two orders of toasts.

一份培根加煎蛋，一壺咖啡，一份凱薩沙拉和二份吐司。

It will be delivered to your room in 20 minutes.

餐點會在二十分鐘後送達你的房間。

Have a good evening. Good bye.

祝福您有個美好的夜晚,拜拜。

H Thanks a lot. You, too. Bye.

謝謝你,你也是,拜拜。

關鍵單字

fried egg *(n. phr.)*	煎蛋
repeat *(v.)*	重複
bacon *(n.)*	培根
salad *(n)*	沙拉
toast *(n.)*	吐司
deliver *(v.)*	遞送

• Unit 9

遇到麻煩
Getting into Trouble

Amy is asking for the room service on the phone.

艾咪正仕電話中要求客房服務。

A: Amy 艾咪 C: Clerk 職員

C Hi, Room Service. How may I help you?

客房中心您好，您需要什麼服務呢？

A There is a problem with my room, number 601.

這裡是 601 號房，房間有些問題。

C What's the problem, Madam?

請問是什麼問題呢，女士？

A The toilet is clogged up. Now it won't flush.

廁所馬桶阻塞了。現在不能沖水。

C Oh, I'm sorry about that.

喔，真的非常抱歉！

We will send a plumber to fix it immediately.

我們立刻派水管工去修理。

A Besides, the TV screen is rather fuzzy and the reception is poor.

還有，電視畫面模糊不清而且收訊也不清楚。

C We sincerely apologize for any of your inconvenience.

造成你的不便我們向你致歉。

We will send a mechanic to repair the TV.

我們會派技工去修理電視。

關鍵單字

toilet *(n.)*	馬桶
clog up *(v. phr.)*	堵塞
flush *(v.)*	沖水
plumper *(n.)*	水電工
immediately *(adv.)*	立刻地
fuzzy *(adj.)*	模糊的
reception *(n.)*	收訊
mechanic *(n.)*	技工
apologize *(v.)*	抱歉
inconvenience *(n.)*	不便利
repair *(v.)*	修理

·Unit 10

轉接電話
Transferring Phone Calls

Amy is salesperson from Japan.
艾咪是一位來自日本的業務人員。

She comes to Taiwan for a business trip.
她來台灣出差。

Now, she is making a phone call to Candy Hotel.
現在她打電話到糖果飯店。

O: Operator 接線生 A: Amy 艾咪

O This is Candy Hotel. How may I help you?
這裡是糖果飯店,請問需要什麼服務呢?

A May I have extension 111 Conference Room, please?
請接分機號111會議室?

O Triple One?
三個一嗎?

A Yes, please.
是的,麻煩您。

O Sorry, the line is busy.
很抱歉，此線忙線中。

A Could you transfer to the room again?
再麻煩你再轉接一次嗎？

O Please hold and I'll check and see if the line is connected.
請現在等候我需確認線路是否有接通。

G Thank you.
謝謝。

關鍵單字

extension *(n.)*	分機(電話)
conference *(n.)*	會議
triple *(adj.)*	三次的，三倍的
transfer *(v.)*	轉接
connect *(v.)*	接通

•Unit 11

找房客
Looking for Occupiers

Amy is a salesperson from Japan.
艾咪是一位來自日本的業務人員。

She comes to Taiwan for a business trip.
她來台灣出差。

Now, she is going to Candy Hotel to look for her friend, Hulk.
現在她到糖果飯店找她的朋友，浩克。

C: Clerk 職員 A: Amy 艾咪

C Welcome to Candy Hotel. How may I help you?
歡迎到糖果飯店，請問你需要什麼服務呢？

A Yes, could you tell me which room Hulk is in, please?
有的，麻煩你。能否告訴我浩克住幾號房嗎？

He is with a tour. But I don't know the name of it.
他是跟旅行團，但是我不知道團名。

I'm his auntie. I happen to know that he stays here.

我是他的阿姨。剛巧知道他今晚入住這裡。

C Excuse me. May I ask what his name is again, please?

抱歉，再次詢問他的大名叫什麼呢？

A Hulk. Hulk Brown.

浩克。浩克布朗。

C Thank you, sir. Just a moment, please.

謝謝您，請稍等。

Mr. Brown is in room 802.

布朗先生住在802房間。

A Where can I call him?

我在哪裡可以打電話給他呢？

C You may use the hotel phone or that public phone booth by the elevator.

你可以使用旅館內線電話，或是電梯旁的公共電話亭。

關鍵單字

look for *(v. phr.)*	尋找
occupier *(n.)*	入住者
colleague *(n.)*	同事
tour *(n.)*	旅行團
happen *(v.)*	剛巧、碰巧
phone booth *(n. phr.)*	電話亭

050

• Unit 12

飯店設施 (1)
Looking for the Facilities (I)

Amy, a business person from Japan, is asking for the health and fitness center at Smile Hotel.

艾咪，來自日本的業務，正在找尋微笑旅館的健身中心。

A: Amy 艾咪 C: Clerk 職員

A Excuse me, where is the swimming pool?
抱歉，請問游泳池在哪裡呢？

C It is on the first basement floor.
它位在地下一樓。

A What time does the swimming pool close?
請問它的開放時間到什麼呢？

C It closes at 10 p.m.
它十點整關閉。

A Is the gymnasium nearby?
請問健身房也在附近嗎？

C It is on the second basement floor.
它位在地下二樓。

A What body-building apparatus are there?
那裡有什麼健身器材可以使用呢？

C Sorry, I don't have a clear idea about it.
抱歉，我不清楚。

But you may contact the staff of the
health and fitness center.
但你可以連絡健身中心的職員。

Or you may go to the health and fitness
center to check it for yourself.
或是直接去健身中心看看。

Our instructors are very happy to help
you.
健身中心的指導員會非常樂意協助你。

關鍵單字

health and fitness center *(n. phr.)*		健身中心
basement *(n.)*		地下室
apparatus *(n.)*		設備;儀器
instructor *(n.)*		指導員

051

• Unit 13

飯店設施 (2)
Looking for the Facilities (Ⅱ)

Amy is asking a clerk for the facilities in the hotel.
艾咪正在問職員關於飯店設施的事情。

A: Amy 艾咪　C: Clerk 職員

A Wait a moment. I'd like to go to the beauty salon.
等等，我想去美容院。

Could you point the direction for me?
你可以幫我指引方向嗎？

C Turn right at the corner.
在那個街角右轉就到了。

Amy is entering to the beauty salon.
艾咪進入美容院。

C Hello, I am glad to help you.
您好，很高興為您服務。

Do you prefer any particular designer?
請問有指定設計師嗎？

A No, I want to have a shampoo and a haircut.

沒有，我要洗頭加剪髮。

C Okay, please take a seat.

好的，請坐。

I am glad to serve you right away.

我隨後幫你服務。

關鍵單字	
shampoo *(n.)*	洗頭
haircut *(n.)*	剪頭

052

•Unit 14

其他飯店服務 (1)
Looking for Other Hotel Services（I）

Hulk is an exchange student from the U.K.
浩克是來自英國的一位交換學生。

He is travelling around Taiwan now.
他現在正在台灣四處旅行。

H: Hulk 浩克 F.R.: Front Reception 櫃台部

F.R. This is Front Reception. How can I help you?
這裡是櫃台部，請問您需要什麼服務呢？

H Hello, I am in room 802.
您好，我是802的房客。

I am wondering if you could help me book one THSR ticket to Zuoyong at 10 a.m. tomorrow morning.

不知可不可以幫我訂一張明天早上十點到左營的高鐵車票？

F.R. Sure, Mr. Brown.

當然可以，布朗先生。

After we made the reservation, we will send you the ticket details.

我們完成訂票後，會通知您並告知相關訂票細節。

You can pick it up at the station tomorrow.

您明天就可以到高鐵車站取票。

H Thanks.

謝謝。

053

•Unit 15

其他飯店服務 (2)
Looking for Other Hotel Services (Ⅱ)

Hulk Brown is asking a clerk at the front reception for other hotel services.

浩克布朗正在詢問櫃台職員關於其他飯店服務的事情。

H: Hulk 浩克 F.R.: Front Reception 櫃台部

H By the way, could you give me some information about the one-day sightseeing tour of the city?

另外，能告訴我市區觀光一日遊的相關資訊嗎？

F.R. Okay, which tour are you interested?

請問您對哪種行程比較感興趣？

H Everything will do. But I don't want to go too far.

任何一種都行，但我不想走太遠的地方。

台北PAPAGO
跟老外介紹台北

F.R. I see. I'll try to provide some places nearby for your reference.

我知道了。盡量提供附近的場所給你參考選擇。

H Thank you. I really appreciate it.

謝謝，非常感謝你。

F.R. You are welcome.

不客氣。

關鍵單字

appreciate *(v.)*　　　感激

Unit 16

退房 (1)
Check-out（Ⅰ）

A: Amy 艾咪 F. R.: Front Reception 櫃台部

F.R. Good morning, Madam. May I help you?
早安，女士。有什麼地方能為你效勞的？

A Yes, I would like to know what time I have to check out.
請問一下退房時間是幾點。

Is it possible that I put off my check-out until 3 p.m.?
我可以延到下午三點之後退房嗎？

F.R. Hi, Madam, our check-out time is usually before 11 a.m..
女士您好，我們的退房時間通常是早上11點前。

Check-out delay would be charged.
延後退房會另收取費用。

A I see. I'll think about it. Thank you.
了解了，我再考慮看看。謝謝。

Unit 17

退房 (2)
Check-out (Ⅱ)

A half hour later, Amy calls the reception.
半小時後。艾咪打給櫃檯。

A: Amy 艾咪 F. R.: Front Reception 櫃台部

A Hello, I'd like to pay the bill.
先生您好我要結帳。

F.R. It will take about 3 minutes to bring you the bill.
請等三分鐘就替您的帳單結算出來。

Your bill comes to a total of NT $ 27,200.
住宿費一共是二萬七千二百元。

A One night costs NT $ 8,400.
一晚住宿費用是八千四百元。

So the total amount should be NT $ 25,200.
所以總共費用應該是二萬五千二百元。

What is the other NT $ 2000 charged for?
其餘的兩千元是甚麼費用呢？

F.R. It's for the room service you ordered on the first night you check in.

這是您在入住第一晚點了房間服務的費用。

A I see. OK. I'm going to check out now.

我了解了。我現在要退房了。

Would you send someone up to room 601 for my luggage?

請問可以派人來601房幫我提行李嗎？

F.R. Sure, how many luggage do you have?

沒問題。請問您有幾件行李呢？

A Two suitcases.

兩件行李箱。

F.R. I will ask a bellhop to take your luggage.

我會通知行李員將您的行李拖到樓下。

We look forward to your next stay with us.

下次期待再度光臨。

A Okay, I will.

好的，我會的。

關鍵單字

bill *(n.)*	帳單
stay *(n.)*	留宿

飯店常用單字

職業(occupation)

行李員 bellhop / porter
門房 doorman / concierge
行李員 duty manager
櫃台人員 receptionist
店員 clerk

設施(facility)

大廳 lobby
前台 reception
電腦房門卡 bin card
行李推車 luggage cart
宴會廳 banquet room
三溫暖 sauna / spa
空調 air condition
洗衣中心 laundry center
健身中心 fitness center
游泳池 swimming pool
美容院 beauty salon
吧台區 bar

Part 2

在民宿

Bed And Breakfast

Taipei is so fun!

• Unit 1

尋找民宿 (1)

Looking for a Bed And Breakfast (I)

Hulk is an exchange student from the U. K. Freya is his host mother in Taiwan.

浩克是從英國來的交換學生。芙蕾雅是他的寄宿家庭母親。

They are having a small talk now.

他們現在正在聊天。

H: Hulk 浩克　F: Freya 芙蕾雅

H I want to go to visit Yilan, but the website says that every hotel there is fully booked.

我想去宜蘭看看，但網站顯示那裡的飯店都已經被訂滿了。

Where else can I find a place to stay?
我還可以去哪裡找地方住宿嗎？

F You could choose B&B instead.
你可選擇民宿。

It's much cheaper.
它比較便宜。

Some B&Bs even give discount during weekdays.
甚至有些民宿提供平日住宿優惠。

H How can I find one?
我要去哪裡找呢？

F First, get online. Check the location you wish to stay.
首先，上網。確認一下你想要入住的地點。

There might be a lot of B&Bs online which are near the place where you are going to visit.
網路上可能會有很多民宿。在你要去的地方附近。

So you might take the distance from a bus station into consideration.

所以你可能要把到達客運站的距離考慮進去。

H That's a good idea. But I worry that the room might be too small.

那是個好主意。但是我擔心民宿的房間會太小。

F On their websites, you could see the introductions and the pictures of their rooms and bathrooms.

在他們的網頁上,可以看到房間與浴室的介紹及照片。

H That's cool!

真是酷喔!

關鍵單字

B&B (Bed and Breakfast) *(n. phr.)* 民宿

weekdays *(n. pl.)* 周間日(周一到周五的日子)

take N into consideration *(v. phr.)* 考慮…

057

Unit 2

尋找民宿 (2)
Looking for a Bed And Breakfast (Ⅱ)

Hulk is an exchange student from the U. K. Freya is his host mother in Taiwan.
浩克是從英國來的交換學生。芙蕾雅是他的寄宿家庭母親。

Hulk is asking Freya about B&Bs in Taiwan.
浩克正在詢問芙蕾雅台灣的民宿訊息。

H: Hulk 浩克 F: Freya 芙蕾雅

H How do I know if the B&B has the basic facilities I need or not?
我要怎麼知道民宿有沒有提供我所需要的基本設備呢？

F You'll need to confirm the dates and keep a list of the B&Bs you are interested in first.
首先，你需要確認好日期及你有興趣入住的民宿名單。

And then call the hosts to see if there's still vacancy and if they have everything you want.

然後打電話給民宿主人，確認是否有空房，是否有提供你想要的設施或服務。

H In that case, guess I have some searching work to do now.

這樣的話，我大概有一些搜尋工作要做了。

Many thanks!

謝謝喔！

F By the way, if a room is available, you normally have to transfer the down payment to confirm your booking.

順帶一提，如果當日有空房，你通常需要先轉帳付訂金來確認你的訂房。

H Hmm... that's new. I'll keep that in mind.

嗯，第一次聽到。我會記住的。

Thanks again for your help!

再次謝謝你的幫忙喔！

F You are welcome! Wish you have a good time in Yilan!

不用客氣。祝你在宜蘭玩得愉快。

058

• Unit 3

電話預約 (1)

Making a Room Reservation by Phone (Ⅰ)

Hulk, an exchange student from the U. K., is making a phone call to reserve a room in a B&B.

浩克，一位英國來的交換學生，正打電話預訂民宿房間。

H: Hulk 浩克 N: Nina 妮娜

N Good afternoon, Luke's B&B. This is Nina speaking.

午安，這裡是路克民宿，我是妮娜。

How may I help you?

有什麼事情可以為您效勞的地方？

H Hello, I am wondering how much it costs to book a double room at your B&B for three days.

您好，我想問訂你們民宿雙人房三天要多少錢？

N If you stay on holidays, it is NT $ 2,580 per night.

假設你選擇在假日入住，每晚是兩千五百八十元新台幣。

On weekdays, it's NT $ 2,080 per night.

若是選擇平日入住，每晚則要兩千零八十元整。

H OK. I'd like to book a double room from June 5 to June 7.

好的。我要預訂六月五日到六月七日一間雙人房。

N Let me check the reservation book. Please hold on.

好的，先生。讓我確認一下登記表，請稍候。

Yes, we still have a double room on June 5 to June 7.

我們在六月五號到七號還有一間雙人房。

H Great! I'll take it!

太好了。我要訂下來。

N No problem.

沒問題。

訂房英文：房間種類

單人房 single room

套房 suite

雙人房(兩張床)twin room

雙人房(一張大床)double room

3 人床客房 trip room

四人房 quad room

家庭房 family room

團體房 group chamber

豪華套房 deluxe suite

總統套房 presidential suite

禁菸房 non-smoking room

獨棟小屋 cabin

男女分開的通舖 female/male dorm

男女混合的通舖 mixed dorm

露營區 camp site

客戶房中沙發可伸縮變為床鋪者
studio (couch, sofa bed)

4 至 6 人同住共有式的住房 condominium

• Unit 4

電話預約 (2)

Making a Room Reservation by Phone (Ⅱ)

Hulk, an exchange student from the U. K., is making a phone call to reserve a room in a B&B.

浩克，一位英國來的交換學生，正打電話預訂民宿房間。

H: Hulk 浩克 N: Nina 妮娜

N Well, you want to reserve one double room from June 5 to June 7.

嗯，你想要預訂六月五日到六月七日一間雙人房。

May I have your name and phone number, please?

請給我你的名字和電話好嗎？

H Sure, my name is Hulk Brown. Phone number is 0953-414243.

當然，我的名字是浩克布朗。電話號碼是 0953-414243。

N Mr. Brown, could you please transfer NT $ 2,000 as a down payment to complete the booking?

布朗先生，可以請您先預付兩千元當作訂金以確認訂房嗎？

I'll text you the transfer details later.

我待會兒會傳簡訊告知您轉帳帳號資料。

H Of course, I'll do it after I get the text.

沒問題，我收到簡訊就會去付款。

And do you provide any special activities for guests?

你們有提供什麼特殊活動讓房客體驗嗎？

N We have some country tour.

我們有提供一些鄉鎮導覽。

Or, you may experience farm work.

不然你也可以體驗農作。

H It sounds fun. I'm looking forward to visiting you soon.

聽起來很有趣。期待能快點拜訪您。

N Please contact me if you have any further questions.

如果您有任何問題，可以再和我連絡。

關鍵單字

detail *(n.)*	細節
provide *(v.)*	提供
experience *(v.)*	體驗

060

Part 3

住在其他的地方

Other than Hotels

Taipei is so fun!

• Unit 1

在青年旅社
In a Hostel

B: Backpacker 背包客 L: Local 當地人

B Sorry, I am new to this town.
抱歉打擾了，我沒來過這個城鎮。

I am looking for a cheap accommodation here.
我正在找便宜的住宿地方。

Is there any place you recommend?
請問有推薦哪裡嗎？

L How about the hostel over there?
那邊那間青年旅館如何？

It is cheap and safe.
那裡既便宜又安全。

Besides, it is near the train station and many shops are within reach.
此外，那裡近火車站而且旁邊又有許多商店。

B Sounds nice. Is there anything special around the hostel?

聽起來不錯。青年旅館附近還有甚麼特別的嗎？

L There are some attractions, fairs and night markets around.

附近有觀光景點、市集及夜市，

You won't feel bored at night.

你不會覺得無聊。

Moreover, you can make friends with people from around the world.

然後，你又可以跟世界各地的人交朋友。

Their staff can speak both English and Japanese.

他們員工都會說英文及日文。

L They also offer pick-up service at the airport.

他們也提供機場接送服務。

B That would be great. Thanks.

那真是太好了。謝謝。

台北PAPAGO
跟老外介紹台北

關鍵單字

attraction *(n.)*	觀光景點
hostel *(n.)*	青年旅館
make friends *(v. phr.)*	交朋友

訂房英文：住宿種類

渡假中心 resort
飯店、旅館 hotel/boutique hotel
小旅店 inn/lodge/cabin
汽車旅館 motel
廉價旅舍 hostel
青年旅館 youth hostel
膠囊旅館 capsule hotel
民宿 B & B hotel (bed and breakfast)/
guest house/pension
短期出租公寓 apartment

061

• Unit 2

汽車旅館
In a Motel

G: Guest 客人 F: Front Desk 櫃台

F Welcome to Smile Motel.
歡迎蒞臨微笑汽車旅館。

Are you staying for rest or for accommodation?
您是要休息還是住宿呢？

G For rest.
我要休息。

F A room with a garage is NT $ 1,280.
休息三小時含附停車位是新台幣一千二百八十元整。

You can stay for three hours.
可以休息三小時。

The screen shows the room photos for your reference.
電腦螢幕顯示房間照片供您選擇參考使用。

Room 301, 303, 305 are still available.
301、303、305號房目前都是空房，

Which one do you prefer?
請問您想要哪一間？

G I choose this room.
我選這間。

F Room 305.
305號房。

Would you like to pay in cash or by credit card?
您要付現還是刷卡。

G In cash.
我要付現。

F Thank you. Here is your key.
謝謝。這是您的鑰匙。

Please go straight to the end, and you will see the room on your right.
請往前直走到底，房間在您右手邊。

Have a nice stay.
祝您愉快。

After two and half hours, the phone rings.
大約兩個小時之後，電話鈴聲響起。

F There are 30 minutes left.
您還有30分休息時間，

Would you need a late chcck-out?
請問有需要另加時間嗎？

G No, I don't. Thank you.
不需要，謝謝。

關鍵單字

accommodation *(n.)*	住宿
garage *(n.)*	車庫
reference *(n.)*	參考

• Unit 3

借住友人家

In a Friend's Place

Phone rings.
電話鈴響

H: Host 主人　F: Friends 友人

F Hi, I know it's late.
我知道很晚了。

I'm sorry to call you at midnight.
很抱歉半夜打給你。

H It's okay. It is New Year's Eve.
沒關係啦！今晚是跨年夜。

My family and I are still awake.
我的家人跟我都還醒著。

F Hey! Say "Happy New Year" to them for me!
嘿！幫我跟他們說一聲「新年快樂」！

H Thank you! Happy New Year to you, too!
謝啦！也祝你新年快樂喔！

Did you have a good time in Taipei today?
你今天在台北玩得愉快嗎？

F Yeah, it's pretty cool!
挺不錯的！

But I did something silly.
但是我做了一件蠢事。

H What happened?
怎麼了？

F I forgot to make a reservation in advance.
我忘記事先訂房。

Now, all the hotels and motels in the city are fully booked.
現在城裡的旅館和汽車旅館都已客滿。

Could I stay at your house tonight?
今晚可以先暫住你家一晚嗎？

H Stay at my place?
住在我家嗎?

F Yes, please. It's New Year's Eve.
對啊,拜託。現在是新年除夕耶。

H Did you bring your toothbrush, towel, and slippers with you?
你有帶著你的牙刷、毛巾跟拖鞋嗎?

F I have my toothbrush and towel.
我帶了牙刷跟毛巾。

But I don't have slippers. Why?
但是我沒有帶拖鞋。為什麼這麼問?

H So that I know what else I have to prepare for you.
這樣我才知道要幫你準備甚麼東西。

F Wow! Does that mean yes?
哇!那是指我可以去借住的意思嗎?

H Yes, bring your baggage.
好吧。帶你的行李過來吧。

F Thank you for your help.
謝謝你的幫忙。

I will clean up the room before I leave.
我離開前會清潔房間的。

H No next time.
下不為例。

• Unit 4

沙發客
Go Couch Surfing

H: Host 主人　F: Friend 友人

F What is couch surfing on earth?
究竟什麼是沙發客？

H It means that you can get a free stay in the journey.
那是指說你可以在旅途中得到免費住宿。

F Awesome! Tell me more!
太棒了！再多告訴我一些！

H If you go couch surfing, you have to post where you travel on the official website before you start.
如果你玩沙發客，你在出發前必須把你要去哪裡旅行公告在官方網站上。

Besides, you have to post the dates when you travel.
此外，你也要公佈你旅遊的日期。

Then, a host in your destination will offer you a sofa in the living room or a room for free.

然後，你目的地的某位主人就會免費提供客廳沙發或是房間給你。

H But you'll have to provide your place for free on the website.

但你也必須免費提供你的住處。

If anyone is coming to visit your city, they will contact you.

如果有人要來拜訪你的城市，他們會跟你聯繫。

F That's cool.

這好酷喔！

Do you know how to become a member of couch surfing?

那你知道要怎麼成為沙發客的一員？

H I remember that you have to register on their official website.

我記得要在他們的官方網站在註冊。

It is not a difficult thing to do, but we have to respect the host's opinion and regulations.

登入操作不難，但必須尊重主人的意願與遵守規定。

F I think I'll give it a try someday. Thank you!

我想我有天要來試看看。謝謝囉!

關鍵單字

couch *(n.)* 沙發

sofa *(n.)* 沙發

surf *(v.)* 衝浪

題外話:

沙發衝浪

沙發衝浪(couch surfing)是由一個美國人凱西范頓(Casey Fenton)所發想的新旅遊住宿方式。有一年他要從波士頓到冰島旅行時,他想找個可以免費借宿的地方。他從他手上有的冰島大學學生電郵中寄了 1500 封詢問免費住宿的信件,出乎意料地,他在 24 小時內收到了 50-100 封的回覆信邀請他前往。這次奇異的經驗促使他在 2004 年成立了沙發衝浪網站,讓全世界愛旅遊的人有另一種貼近在地生活的新式住宿方式。

PAPAGO

台灣料理

Taiwanese Food

Taipei is
so fun!

Unit 1

台灣餐廳 (1)
Restaurants in Taiwan (I)

Alina is an exchange student who comes from the U.S.A.
艾琳娜是來自美國的交換學生。

Now, she is talking to her father via Skype.
現在她正在用 SKYPE 跟父親通話。

A: Alina 艾琳娜 D: Dad 父親

A Good morning, Daddy!
早安，老爸!

D Good morning and good afternoon, my sweet girl!
早安跟午安，我的寶貝女兒！

Your mom and I miss you a lot!
妳媽媽跟我都好想妳！

A I miss you a lot, too!
我也好想你們！

How's everything there?
家裡一切都好嗎？

D Good. Don't worry about us!
很好，不用擔心我們！

How are you doing in Taipei?
妳在台北都還好嗎？

A Good! Don't worry about me!
我很好，不用擔心！

You won't believe it!
你們不會相信！

The food here is awcsomc!
這裡的食物很棒！

D Really? I thought you don't like Chinese food！
真的嗎？我以為妳不喜歡中式食物呢！

A I thought I didn't like Chinese food, either!
我以前也以為我不喜歡中式食物！

But the Chinese food here is so different from those we have in America!

但是這裡的食物跟我們在美國吃到的中式食物比起來很不一樣！

D What is the difference?

怎麼不一樣？

Don't they eat rice or noodles?

他們不是吃飯跟麵嗎？

A Yes, they do. But food in Taipei is tasty and fresh.

是，但是台北的食物很美味又很新鮮。

Besides, food here is less oily and less expensive!

而且比較不油，又比較便宜！

D That sounds good.

聽起不錯喔！

關鍵單字	
tasty *(adj.)*	美味的
fresh *(adj.)*	新鮮的

• Unit 2

台灣餐廳 (2)
Restaurants in Taiwan (Ⅱ)

Alina is an exchange student who comes from the U.S.A.

艾琳娜是來自美國的交換學生。

Now, she is introducing food in Taipei to her father via Skype.

現在她正在 SKYPE 上跟父親介紹台北的食物。

A: Alina 艾琳娜 D: Dad 父親

A And the restaurants in Taipei are interesting, too.

而且台北的餐廳也好有趣。

D What do you mean?

你的意思是?

A They got all kinds of restaurants everywhere, from fancy restaurants, Chinese buffets, to food stands in the night markets.

到處都有各式各樣的餐廳,從昂貴的餐廳、中式自助餐廳,到夜市的路邊攤都有。

D Cool. But what is "Chinese buffet"?
酷喔! 什麼是中式自助餐廳?

A Ha! That's the most interesting part.
哈! 那是最有趣的部分!

When I first walked into a Chinese
buffet, I was so confused.
第一次走進中式自助餐廳的時候,我非常困
惑。

D Confused? Why?
困惑? 為什麼?

A Everyone is picking up food from big
trays to his or her lunch box or paper
plate by tongs.
每一個人都在用夾子從大餐盤上面夾菜到自
己的便當盒或紙餐盤上。

I didn't know where to get the tongs and
a lunch box.
我不知道要去哪裡拿夾子跟便當空盒。

Then a person helped me by pointing out the direction.

然後，有一個顧客指出方向來幫我。

D Hmm, you are lucky!

嗯，運氣不錯喔！

A Well, people here are quite friendly.

這裡的人都蠻友善的！

關鍵單字

fancy *(adj.)*	新奇的、昂貴的
Chinese buffet *(n. phr.)*	中式自助餐
tray *(n.)*	餐盤
paper plate *(n.)*	紙餐盤
tongs *(n. pl.)*	夾子

• Unit 3

台灣餐廳 (3)
Restaurants in Taiwan (Ⅲ)

Alina is an exchange student who comes from the U.S.A.

艾琳娜是來自美國的交換學生。

Now, she is talking to her father via Skype and comparing a Chinese buffet with an all-you-can-eat buffet.

現在她正在 SKYPE 上跟父親聊天，並比較中式自助餐廳與吃到飽餐廳。

A: Alina 艾琳娜 D: Dad 父親

D Was there anything particular in the Chinese buffet?

在那中式自助餐廳還有發生甚麼事嗎？

A Oh, right! Yes!

對！還有！

When I finished picking up the food and was about to start my lunch, a lady stopped me and told me to pay first!

我夾完我要吃的菜並準備要開動時，一個女士阻止我，跟我說要先付錢。

D Hadn't you paid the bill before you picked up your food?

你在夾菜之前，沒有先付錢嗎？

A No, I didn't. It's not a typical all-you-can-it buffet.

沒有，因為那不是典型的吃到飽餐廳。

Here, you have to pick up what you want first and the clerk will help you weigh your food and charge you accordingly.

在這裡，你先夾好你要吃的菜，然後店員會秤食物，然後依據重量算價錢。

D I see.

我懂了。

A Except that, the rest is almost like an all-you-can-eat buffet.

除了此之外，其他部分就幾乎跟吃到飽餐廳一樣了。

D What do you mean by saying "almost"?
你説「幾乎」是甚麼意思？

A A Chinese buffet serves a variety of dishes, noodles and dumplings for diners to choose from.
中式自助餐廳提供很多樣化的餐點、麵條、餃子供客人選擇。

However, there seems to be few desserts in a Chinese buffet.
但是幾乎沒有甚麼甜點。

D Ha! What a pity! You have sweet tooth.
哈！可惜了! 你愛吃甜食！

A You know me well, daddy!
老爸，你真了解我！

關鍵單字

all-you-can-eat buffet *(n.)*	吃到飽餐廳
sweet tooth *(n. phr.)*	愛吃甜食的偏好

067

Unit 4

火鍋 (1)
Chinese Hot Pot (I)

Alina is an exchange student who comes from the U.S.A.
艾琳娜是來自美國的交換學生。

Now, she is talking to her mother via Skype.
現在她正在 SKYPE 上跟母親聊天。

A: Alina 艾琳娜 M: Mom 母親

Ⓐ Mom! You won't believe this!
媽！你不會相信的！

Ⓜ What is it, my sweetie?
甚麼事情？

Ⓐ I cooked Chinese food today!
我今天煮了中式料理。

Ⓜ Really? Who taught you?
真的嗎？是誰教你的呢？

A My friend, Eric.
我朋友艾利克。

I met him in the Chinese lesson. Remember?
我們在中文課上認識的。記得嗎？

M Yes, I remember. He is cute!
我記得，他很可愛。

But I didn't know he can cook Chinese food.
我不知道他會煮中式料理耶。

A Ha! No, he can't!
哈！他不會煮啊！

He took me to a Chinese hot pot restaurant.
他帶我去火鍋餐廳。

M Chinese hot pot?
火鍋？

A Yes, Chinese hot pot!
是的，火鍋！

068

Unit 5

火鍋 (2)
Chinese Hot Pot (Ⅱ)

Alina is an exchange student who comes from the U.S.A.
艾琳娜是來自美國的交換學生。

Now, she is introducing Chinese hot pot to her mother via Skype.
現在她正在 SKYPE 上跟母親介紹火鍋。

A: Alina 艾琳娜 M: Mom 母親

M What is that? How do you make it?
那是什麼？你們怎麼料理？

A We were served with soup in a small pot first.
我們剛開始拿到一小鍋湯。

Later, we got a tray of raw meat slices and vegetables.
然後，拿到一盤生肉片跟蔬菜。

M Raw meat and uncooked vegetables?
生肉跟生的蔬菜？

A Yes. Mom, your reaction sounds so funny!
沒錯。媽，你的反應聽起來好好笑！

We did not eat those uncooked food.
我們沒吃生食。

We put them into the soup.
我們將它們放進湯裡面。

M But they are raw!
但是它們是生的耶！

A Yes, so we have to turn on the induction cooker which is underneath the hot pot.
對，所以我們必須要把火鍋下面的電磁爐打開。

And we cook the raw meat slices and vegetables all by ourselves.
然後自己把生肉跟蔬菜煮熟。

M I see. But why don't they cook for you?
我懂了，但是他們為什麼不幫你煮好？

A I don't know! But I think it's more fun to cook the food by ourselves.
我不知道，但是自己煮比較有趣啊！

hot pot *(n. phr.)*	火鍋
raw *(adj.)*	生的、未煮熟的
meat slice *(n. phr.)*	肉片
induction cooker *(n. phr.)*	電磁爐

火鍋常用單字

醬料 (Sauce)

蒜泥 mashed garlic

醬油 soy sauce

蘿蔔泥 mashed daikon

醬油膏 oyster sauce

沙茶醬 barbecue sauce

香椿醬 Chinese toon sauce

薑末 mashed ginger

辣椒醬 chili sauce

蔬菜(Vegetables)

青江菜 spoon cabbage

紅蘿蔔 carrot

高麗菜 cabbage

山藥 Chinese yam

白菜 bok choy

南瓜 pumpkin

大陸妹 Taiwanese lettuce

白木耳 white fungus

秋葵 okra

黑木耳 black fungus

069

• Unit 6

火鍋 (3)
Chinese Hot Pot (Ⅲ)

Alina is an exchange student who comes from the U.S.A.

艾琳娜是來自美國的交換學生。

Now, she is introducing what hot pot is to her mother via Skype.

現在她正在 SKYPE 上跟母親介紹什麼是火鍋。

A: Alina 艾琳娜 M: Mom 母親

M Did the hot pot taste nice?
吃起來好吃嗎？

A It was delicious! And we got to make our own dipping.
好吃！而且我們可以自己製作自己的沾醬

M How?
怎麼做？

A There were different sauces, ingredients, spices at a corner of the restaurant.
在餐廳的一個角落有不同的醬料、材料與香料。

We could choose what we would like and mix them up.

我們可以選擇我們想要什麼並將它們混在一起。

Ⓜ It seems very interesting.

好像很有趣。

What did you put in your own dipping?

你放了甚麼在你的沾醬裡？

Ⓐ I put BBQ sauce and ginger.

我放了沙茶醬跟薑。

Ⓜ How was it?

嚐起來如何？

Ⓐ Well, it's a little weird, but nice.

有一點怪，但是還不錯。

Ⓜ Well, I'm glad you learn to cook now!

嗯，我很高興你開始學煮東西了！

關鍵單字

spice (n.)	香料
ingredient (n.)	食材
dipping (n.)	沾醬
weird (adj.)	怪異的

070

• Unit 7

台灣麵食 (1)
Noodles in Taiwan (Ⅰ)

Alina, Eric and Lily are exchange students from the U.S.A.
艾琳娜、艾力克和莉莉是從美國來的交換學生。

They are classmates in a Chinese Culture Class in Taipei now.
他們現在在台北是同一個中國文化課的同學。

A: Alina 艾琳娜 E: Eric 艾力克 L: Lily 莉莉

A I can't believe Mr. Chen asked us to do a report on Taiwanese food!
我不敢相信陳老師竟然要我們做台灣食物的報告！

E Why not? I am quite interested in it!
為什麼？我還蠻感興趣的耶！

A But I've just got here for two weeks!
我才剛到這裡兩個禮拜！

I know nothing about Taiwanese food!
我對台灣食物一竅不通！

L Alina, don't worry! Eric and I will help you!
艾琳娜，不用擔心！艾力克跟我會幫妳的！

E Yeah, Alina, don't panic!
對啊，艾琳娜，不用驚慌啦！

What's your topic?
你的主題是甚麼？

A I need to introduce Taiwanese noodles.
我要介紹台灣的麵食。

L Ha! That's my favorite!
哈！那是我的最愛耶！

A Really? I only know egg noodles.
真的嗎？我只知道雞蛋麵！

L Well, egg noodles are our stereotype about Chinese noodles in America.
雞蛋麵是我們在美國對於中國麵食的刻版印象。

Taiwanese noodles are way more various than that!
台灣的麵食比那個還要有變化多了！

report *(n.)*	報告
panic *(v.)*	驚慌
topic *(n.)*	主題
egg noodles *(n. phr.)*	雞蛋麵

• Unit 8

台灣麵食 (2)
Noodles in Taiwan (Ⅱ)

Alina, Eric and Lily are classmates in the same Chinese Culture Class.
艾琳娜、艾力克和莉莉是同一個中國文化課的同學。

They are discussing their reports about Chinese noodles in Taiwan now.
他們正在討論台灣中式麵條的報告。

A: Alina 艾琳娜 E: Eric 艾力克 L: Lily 莉莉

E Here in Taipei, you can see a variety of noodles.
在台北，你可以看見各種麵條。

There are fried noodles, soup noodles, dry noodles, cold noodles, and my favorite, instant noodles !
他們有炒麵、湯麵、乾麵、涼麵，和我的最愛，泡麵！

L Well, Eric, we all know you hide a carton of instant noodles under your bed.

好啦，艾力克。我們都知道你藏了一箱泡麵在你床底下！

E Lily! That's my top secret!

莉莉！那是我的最高機密耶！

A Haha! You keep your hidden instant noodles as your top secret!

哈哈！你把藏起來的泡麵當作你的最高機密！

E Thanks, Lily. Now everybody knows my secret!

謝啦，莉莉。現在大家都知道我的秘密了！

L I'm sorry, Eric.

抱歉啦！艾力克！

關鍵單字	
instant noodles *(n. phr.)*	泡麵
carton *(n.)*	紙箱
top secret *(n. phr.)*	最高機密

072

• Unit 9

台灣麵食 (3)
Noodles in Taiwan (Ⅲ)

Alina, Eric and Lily are classmates in the same Chinese Culture Class.
艾琳娜、艾力克和莉莉是同一個中國文化課的同學。

They are discussing their reports about Chinese noodles in Taiwan now.
他們正在討論台灣中式麵條的報告。

A: Alina 艾琳娜 E: Eric 艾力克 L: Lily 莉莉

A What are cold noodles?
什麼是涼麵？

E The noodles are meant to be cold when they are served.
麵端上來時，是冰冰涼涼的！

A That's really cool!
那真是酷涼啊！

I bet it feels great to have some for lunch in summer.
我猜夏天午餐吃這個一定感覺超棒的！

L They are usually served with sesame sauce and some vegetables.

涼麵通常都是跟芝麻醬還有一些青菜一起吃。

E The sesame sauce is the key element!

芝麻醬是關鍵！

It smells so great!

聞起來超香的！

And you can buy cool noodles in convenience stores.

而且在便利商店就買得到。

Isn't it great?

很棒吧？

A Wow! It is so convenient!

哇！超方便的！

I definitely need to try some later!

我待會一定要去吃看看！

關鍵單字	
sesame *(n.)*	芝麻
element *(n.)*	要素

073

• Unit 10

台灣麵食 (4)
Noodles in Taiwan (Ⅳ)

Alina, Eric and Lily are classmates in the same Chinese Culture Class.
艾琳娜、艾力克和莉莉是同一個中國文化課的同學。

They are discussing their reports about Chinese noodles in Taiwan now.
他們正在討論台灣中式麵條的報告。

A: Alina 艾琳娜 E: Eric 艾力克 L: Lily 莉莉

A Is there anything else about noodles in Taiwan that I should know?
關於台灣麵食，還有什麼是我需要知道的嗎？

E Oh! The shape of the noodles!
喔！麵條的形狀！

L Right! There are thin noodles, flat noodles, oolong noodles, knife-shaved noodles....
對！有細麵、寬麵、烏龍麵、刀削麵…。

Ⓐ Wait, knife-shaved noodles？That sounds dangerous!

等一下！刀削麵？那聽起來好危險！

Ⓔ Don't worry! It won't taste bloody.

不用擔心！嘗起來不會有血腥味！

To make knife-shaved noodles, chefs shave the dough with knives and let the shaved noodles fall directly into the pot.

要做刀削麵，廚子會用刀削麵團，讓削下的麵團直接落在鍋裡。

Ⓐ Hmm... I might want to take a look.

嗯，我想要看一看。

關鍵單字

bloody *(adj.)*	血腥的
shave *(v.)*	削
dough *(n.)*	麵團

Unit 11

台灣麵食 (5)
Noodles in Taiwan (V)

Alina, Eric and Lily are classmates in the same Chinese Culture Class.
艾琳娜、艾力克和莉莉是同一個中國文化課的同學。

They are discussing their reports about Chinese noodles in Taiwan now.
他們正在討論台灣中式麵條的報告。

A: Alina 艾琳娜 E: Eric 艾力克 L: Lily 莉莉

A Lily, what's your favorite noodles in Taiwan?
莉莉，那你最喜歡的台灣麵食是什麼？

L I would say beef noodles.
我會說是牛肉麵。

You won't find any better noodles in any other place!
你絕對不會在其他地方吃到這麼好吃的麵！

A Oh! I know that!
喔! 我知道!

Eric once took me to have some beef noodles, right?
艾力克，你有一次有帶我去吃過，對嗎?

E Yes, and you asked the boss how to make the dish.
你還問老闆是怎麼做的。

A They told me at least 10 Chinese spices were used to make a serving of beef noodles.
他們說至少要用十種中式香料才能做出一份牛肉麵。

L No wonder the taste and the smell are so rich!
難怪味道及香氣如此豐富!

See, Alina.
看吧，艾琳娜!

You do know something about Taiwanese noodles!
妳是了解台灣麵食的!

• Unit 12

台灣節慶食物 (1)
Chinese Festival Cuisine in Taiwan (I)

Eric and Lily are exchange students from the U.S.A.
艾力克跟莉莉是從美國來的交換學生。

They take the same Chinese Culture course and now they are discussing Chinese Festival Cuisine in Taiwan with their teacher, Mr. Chen.
他們修同一門中華文化課。現在,他們正和陳老師討論台灣節慶食物。

C: Mr. Chen 陳老師　E: Eric 艾力克
L: Lily 莉莉

C You all did great presentations on your Taiwanese food reports.
你們的台灣料理報告都做得很好。

To reward your efforts, we are going to have sweet dumplings today!
為了獎勵你們的努力,我們今天要去吃甜湯圓!

E Mr. Chen, do you mean we are going to make sweet dumplings here, or you are going to take us out to have some?

陳老師，你的意思是指我們要在這裡煮甜湯圓，還是你要帶我們出去吃？

C Hold on, hold on. First thing first.

等等，一件一件來。

I think the question should be why I choose sweet dumplings.

我想問題應該是，我為什麼選甜湯圓。

L Because recently they have been on TV every day?

因為最近電視上天天都看得到？

C Why have we seen them on TV every day recently?

為什麼最近天天出現在電視上？

E Because the Lantern Festival is around the corner!

因為元宵節要到了！

The sweet dumplings look like lanterns in the soup!

甜湯圓看起來像湯裡的燈籠！

C Eric is right about the reason why we are going to have sweet dumplings today.
艾力克說中了今天要吃湯圓的理由。

關鍵單字

reward *(v.)*	獎勵
sweet dumpling *(n. phr.)*	甜湯圓
lantern *(n.)*	燈籠
Lantern Festival *(n. phr.)*	元宵節；燈籠節

Unit 13

台灣節慶食物 (2)
Chinese Festival Cuisine in Taiwan (II)

Eric and Lily are exchange students from the U.S.A.
艾力克跟莉莉是從美國來的交換學生。

They take the same Chinese Culture course and now they are discussing Chinese festival cuisine in Taiwan with their teacher, Mr. Chen.
他們修同一門中華文化課。現在，他們正和陳老師討論台灣節慶食物。

C: Mr. Chen 陳老師 E: Eric 艾力克
L: Lily 莉莉

E I know people here eat different things to celebrate different festivals.
我知道這裡人們吃不同的東西來慶祝不同的節日。

It is sort of a tradition here.
有點兒像是這裡的傳統。

C And that's our next topic!

那正是我們接下來的主題！

Would you like to give us some examples, Eric?

艾力克，你願意幫我們舉一些例子嗎？

E I only know about two.

我只知道兩個。

First, people eat moon cakes on Mid-autumn Festival.

首先，中秋節時吃月餅。

The second is rice dumplings on Dragon Boat Festival.

其次是端午節時的粽子。

C Very good! Very good!

很好！很好！

L Mr. Chen, but why do I see many people here have barbecue on Mid-autumn Festival?

陳老師，為什麼我中秋節看到這裡的人都在烤肉？

C That's because a TV commercial encouraged people to do that a few years ago.

那是因為幾年前有個電視廣告鼓勵大家這麼做。

Later on, it became a new tradition.
然後，烤肉就變成一項新傳統了。

L But they still eat moon cakes, right?
但是他們還是有吃月餅，對嗎？

C Yes, they still do.
對，還是有吃。

關鍵單字

Mid-autumn Festival *(n. phr.)*	中秋節	
Dragon Boat Festival *(n. phr.)*	端午節	
rice dumplings *(n. phr.)*	粽子	
barbecue *(n.)*	烤肉	
commercial *(n.)*	廣告	

Unit 14

台灣節慶食物 (3)
Chinese Festival Cuisine in Taiwan (Ⅲ)

Eric and Lily are exchange students from the U.S.A.
艾力克跟莉莉是從美國來的交換學生。

They take the same Chinese Culture course and now they are discussing Chinese festival cuisine in Taiwan with their teacher, Mr. Chen.
他們修同一門中華文化課。現在,他們正和陳老師討論台灣節慶食物。

C: Mr. Chen 陳老師 E: Eric 艾力克
L: Lily 莉莉

Ⓔ The Chinese festival cuisine in Taiwan is so interesting. Is there anything particular?
台灣節慶食物好有趣喔!還有什麼特別的嗎?

Ⓒ Have you ever tried a kind of sweet and sticky cake?
你們有嚐過一種甜甜的、黏黏的糕點嗎?

L I have! My landlord told me that people here have that in Chinese New Year!
我有！我的房東告訴我中國新年就要吃那個！

C Wow, you have a very hospitable landlord!
哇，你房東很好客耶！

The sweet and sticky cake is called "nian-gao", meaning year cake.
那叫做年糕，意思是過年的糕。

Some call it "rice cake" in English.
有些人翻譯為「米做的糕」。

E Nian-gao. Was it good, Lily?
年糕。那好吃嗎，莉莉？

L Umm... it's sweet and sticky!
嗯，甜甜黏黏的！

關鍵單字	
sticky *(adj.)*	有黏性的
hospitable *(adj.)*	好客的

078

Part 2

亞洲料理

Asian Cuisine

韓式料理 (1)

Korean Cuisine (Ⅰ)

Alina and Eric are exchange students from the U.S.A.
艾琳娜和艾力克是來自美國的交換學生。

They just finished their Chinese Culture course and are ready for lunch.
他們剛結束中華文化課，準備要去吃午餐。

A: Alina 艾琳娜 E: Eric 艾力克

E It's 11:30 now. Are you hungry?
現在11:30了，你餓了嗎？

A Are you kidding? I'm starving!
你開玩笑嗎？我餓死了！

E Starving? Didn't you have your breakfast?
這麼餓？你沒吃早餐嗎？

A I only had a piece of toast.
我只吃了一片吐司。

E No wonder. Fancy going to a Korean restaurant with me?
難怪。想跟我一起去韓式料理店吃飯嗎？

A Are there any Korean restaurants here in Taipei?
台北有韓式料理店嗎？

E Well, Taipei is quite an international city.
嗯，台北市個國際的城市。

Of course, there are plenty of Korean restaurants in Taipei.
當然有許多韓式料理店啊。

A That's great! I've always wanted to try Korean kimchi.
那太好了！我一直都很想試看看韓式泡菜。

關鍵單字	
starve *(v.)*	飢餓
no wonder *(n. phr.)*	難怪
fancy *(v.)*	想要
korean kimchi *(n. phr.)*	韓式泡菜

Unit 2

韓式料理 (2)
Korean Cuisine (Ⅱ)

Alina and Eric are exchange students from the U.S.A.

艾琳娜和艾力克是來自美國的交換學生。

They are going to a Korean restaurant for lunch.

他們要去一間韓式料理店用午餐。

A: Alina 艾琳娜 E: Eric 艾力克

E Voila! Here we are.

到啦！就是這裡。

Kimchi may not be the main course in this restaurant.

韓式泡菜可能不是這間餐廳的主菜。

However, I think you may like this one.

但是，我想你應該也會喜歡這間。

Ⓐ Wow! It smells so barbecue!
哇！聞起來好有烤肉味喔！

Ⓔ Welcome to a Korean barbecue restaurant!
歡迎來到韓式烤店！

Let's order some food first!
我們先來點些食物吧！

Ⓐ OK. What would you like to order?
好。你要點甚麼呢？

Ⓔ I would like to have some shrimps,
我想先來點蝦子。

Ⓐ Shrimps for barbecue? That's new for me!
燒烤蝦子？真新奇呢！

Ⓔ Again, welcome to Korean barbecue restaurant!
對啊！歡迎來到韓式燒烤！

The meat and seafood here are marinated with their own unique sauce.
這裡的肉或是海鮮都已經先用獨特的醬料醃製過了。

A That sounds very convenient and
delicious.
聽起來真是非常方便又很好吃的樣子呢！

I can't wait!
我等不及了！

關鍵單字	
shrimp *(n.)*	蝦子
marinate *(v.)*	醃製
unique *(adj.)*	獨特的

• Unit 3

韓式料理 (3)
Korean Cuisine (Ⅲ)

Alina and Eric are exchange students from the U.S.A.
艾琳娜和艾力克是來自美國的交換學生。

They are ordering their foods in a Korean restaurant in Taipei.
他們正在台北某間韓式料理店點餐。

A: Alina 艾琳娜 E: Eric 艾力克
W: Waitress 女服務生

W Are you ready to order?
請問您們要點餐了嗎？

E Yes, I would like a plate of shrimps.
是，我要一盤蝦子。

Alina, what would you like?
艾琳娜，妳想要點甚麼呢？

Ⓐ I would like a plate of pork, please.
我想要一盤豬肉。

May I have some kimchi as well?
我還要些泡菜。

Ⓦ Kimchi, salad and dressings, dipping,
along with fruit are all in the buffet area.
泡菜、生菜、沙拉醬、沾醬跟水果都在自助
餐吧區。

Please help yourself to it.
請自行取用。

Ⓐ I see. Thank you very much.
我懂了。非常謝謝你。

Excuse me. Do you also serve drinks and
desserts?
不好意思，你們有提供飲料跟甜點嗎？

Ⓦ Yes, our drinks are free and you may find
them in the buffet zone.
有的，店內飲料是免費的，你可以在自助餐
吧區。

If you would like some desserts, I'll get
you the dessert menu.
如果您需要甜點的話，我可以送上甜點的菜
單。

A No, thanks.
不，不用了。謝謝。

E That should be enough for now. Thank you.
目前先這樣就好了。謝謝你。

W Sure. I'll leave the menu here.
沒問題，我先把菜單留在這裡。

If you need to order something else, just give me a shout.
如果還需要加點別的，就叫我一聲。

關鍵單字

dressing *(n.)*	沙拉醬
along with *(prep. phr.)*	以及
give someone a shout *(v. phr.)*	叫某人一聲

Unit 4

印度料理 (1)
Indian Cuisine (I)

Alina and Lily are exchange students from the U.S.A.
艾琳娜和莉莉是來自美國的交換學生。

They are having a small talk now.
他們正在聊天。

A: Alina 艾琳娜 L: Lily 莉莉

L So, how's your date?
那麼，約會如何啊？

A What date?
甚麼約會？

L Oh, come on. Eric took you out twice!
喔，拜託！艾利克帶你出去約會兩次了耶！

A Oh, Eric, you mean.
喔，你是說艾利克啊。

He's wonderful.
他很好啊！

The restaurants he introduced me were amazing!

他帶我去吃的餐廳真的超棒的！

L What kind of restaurant?

那一種餐廳？

A A Chinese hot pot restaurant and a Korean barbecue restaurant.

一間中式火鍋店跟一間韓式燒烤餐廳。

L Hmm... so I guess you haven't tried any Indian restaurants here.

嗯，所以我猜你還沒試過這裡的印度料理餐廳？

A Indian restaurants? You mean here in Taipei?

印度餐廳？你是說在台北這裡嗎？

L Yes, Alina.

對，艾琳娜。

A No, I didn't know they have Indian restaurants here.

沒有，我不知道這裡有印度餐廳。

L Welcome to Taipei!

歡迎來到台北！

They've got all kinds of foods and cuisines here!

他們有各式各樣的食物跟料理呢！

Come on. Let's go to an Indian restaurant for dinner now.

走吧！咱們現在去印度餐廳吃晚餐吧！

• Unit 5

印度料理 (2)
Indian Cuisine (Ⅱ)

Alina and Lily are exchange students from the U.S.A.

艾琳娜和莉莉是來自美國的交換學生。

They are having their dinner in an Indian restaurant in Taipei.

他們現在正在台北某間印度餐廳用晚餐。

A: Alina 艾琳娜 L: Lily 莉莉

A Wow! Look at the menu!
哇！你看看這個菜單！

Tandoori chicken, samosa, nan and all kinds of curry！
坦都利烤雞, 咖哩角，烤餅，和各式各樣的咖哩！

It is so Indian!
好印度喔！

L I know! And the chef comes from India!
我知道！而且這裡的主廚來自印度呢！

A What? That is so cool!
甚麼？那真的太酷了！

I want to order everything in the menu.
菜單上的每一樣菜我都想要點來嚐嚐！

L Calm down, Alina. I remember you don't eat any spicy food.
冷靜一點，艾琳娜。我記得你不吃辣的。

A No, I don't. I nearly forget that.
不，我不吃辣，差點忘記了。

L Do you see there's a chili mark on the menu?
你在菜單上有看到辣椒的符號嗎？

It shows how spicy the course is.
它表示那道菜有多辣。

The more chili marks show behind the course, the spicier the course is.
越多辣椒符號在那道菜後面，那道菜就越辣。

A I got it. Guess I'll try one-chili course this time.

了解，我猜我這次先試看看一個辣椒符號的菜好了。

What about drinks? What is "mango lassi"？

那飲料呢？甚麼是「芒果拉西」？

L That is a kind of drink made with yogurt and mango.

那是一種用優格根芒果做的飲料。

You may give it a try. It's special but not too weird.

試看看，它很特別，但是不會太奇怪。

A OK. I'll give it a try.

好，我就來試看看。

Are you ready to order?

你準備好要點餐了嗎？

L Yes, my lady! Ha!

是的，我的大小姐！哈！

關鍵單字

tandoori chicken *(n. phr.)*	坦都利烤雞
samosa *(n.)*	咖哩角
nan *(n.)*	印度烤餅
curry *(n.)*	咖哩
calm down *(v. phr.)*	冷靜
spicy *(adj.)*	辣的
chili *(n.)*	辣椒
mark *(n.)*	符號
course *(n.)*	菜 (主菜)
lassi *(n.)*	拉西(印度酸奶昔)
sour *(adj.)*	酸的
yogurt *(n.)*	優格
mango *(n.)*	芒果

• Unit 6

泰式料理 (1)
Thai Cuisine (I)

Alina, Eric and Lily are exchange students from the U.S. A.
艾琳娜、艾利克和莉莉是來自美國的交換學生。

Now, they are having a small talk in the classroom.
現在，他們正在教室裡聊天。

A: Alina 艾琳娜 E: Eric 艾利克 L: Lily 莉莉

E I can't believe you two went to an Indian restaurant without me.
我真不敢相信你們兩個去印度餐廳居然沒找我！

A I'm sorry, Eric.
艾利克，對不起嘛！

We didn't mean it.
我們不是故意的！

Lily and I were talking about Asian foods here.
莉莉跟我在聊這裡的亞洲食物。

She heard that I hadn't tried any Indian food before.

她聽到我還沒吃過印度料理，

Then, we decided to go on the spur of the moment.

我們就臨時起意就決定要去了。

L Yeah, Eric. Then, let's go to a Thai restaurant for lunch together?

對啊，艾利克。不然，我們午餐一起去吃泰式料理，如何啊？

E Thai cuisine?

泰式料理嗎？

A What? Lily? I haven't been to any Thai restaurants in Taipei!

什麼？莉莉，我還沒去過台北任何一家泰式餐廳耶！

L You are going to know one soon!

你很快就要知道其中一間囉！

Let's go now!

一起走吧！

• Unit 7

泰式料理 (2)
Thai Cuisine (Ⅱ)

Alina, Eric and Lily are exchange students from the U.S.A.

艾琳娜、艾利克和莉莉是來自美國的交換學生。

Now, they are going to a Thai restaurant together for their lunch.

現在,他們正往泰式餐廳,準備要用午餐。

A: Alina 艾琳娜 E: Eric 艾利克
L: Lily 莉莉 W: Waiter 男服務生

L Here we are!
到囉!

E Cool. Lily, you know Taipei better than me.
酷喔!莉莉,妳比我還了解台北耶!

W Sawadeeka!
你好!

L Sawadeeka! Three people, please.
你好!三位,麻煩你了!

W OK. Please follow me.
好的，請跟我來。

A The decoration here is very Thai.
這餐廳的裝飾很泰式耶！

W Yes, most of the furniture and statues here are directly imported from Thailand.
是的，大部分的家具跟雕像都是直接從泰國進口。

E Hmm, very impressive.
嗯，很令人印象深刻。

W Here is the table for three.
這裡是您的三人座位。

Have you been here before?
你們有來過嗎？

L Only me. Please introduce your menu for them.
只有我來過，請向他們介紹一下菜餐。

W No problem.
沒問題。

The starters are on the first two pages and you can select your main courses from page three and four.

前面兩頁是前菜，而第三第四頁是主菜選單。

The last two pages are side dishes, drinks, and desserts.

最後兩頁是附餐、飲料、跟甜點。

The dishes with a crown mark in the front are the most popular ones.

有皇冠符號在前方的餐點是這裡最受歡迎的菜色。

A And I know the ones with a chili mark are spicy!

而且我知道有辣椒符號的菜代表會辣！

L Haha! Yes, we all know that!

哈哈，對，我們都知道！

關鍵單字

Sawadeeka (泰文)	你好
decoration *(n.)*	裝飾
import *(v.)*	進口
furniture *(n.)*	家具
statue *(n.)*	雕像
impressive *(adj.)*	印象深刻的
introduce *(v.)*	介紹
starter *(n.)*	前菜
main course *(n. phr)*	主菜
side dishes *(n. phr.)*	附餐

Unit 8

泰式料理 (3)
Thai Cuisine (Ⅲ)

Alina, Eric and Lily are exchange students from the U.S. A.

艾琳娜、艾利克和莉莉是來自美國的交換學生。

Now, they are ordering food in a Thai restaurant.

現在,他們正在一間泰式餐廳點餐。

A: Alina 艾琳娜 E: Eric 艾利克 L: Lily 莉莉 W: Waiter 男服務生

W Are you ready to order now?

你們準備好要點餐了嗎?

E I think we need to discuss for a bit.

我覺得我們需要討論一下。

W Of course. Let me know when you are ready to order.

當然。準備好要點餐時讓我知道一下。

L The portion of one main course is enough for three of us to share.

一份主餐的量足夠讓我們三個人分著吃。

E We can order three main courses and share with one another.

我們可以點三份主餐，然後彼此分著吃。

A That would be great!

那太棒了！

How about beef with green curry?

綠咖哩牛肉如何？

L That's a bit spicy.

那有一點辣，

If you are OK with it, I would like to try it.

如果你可以的話，我很願意試看看。

E What is Thai curry fish cake?

甚麼是泰式咖哩魚肉餅？

A I don't know. Should we try?

我不知道耶，要試看看嗎？

L Sure! And I feel like to have some deep-fried chicken with hot sauce.

好啊！然後我想嚐嚐泰式椒麻雞。

E Sure! I would like to have a starter, too.
好啊！我還想要點一個前菜。

A Oh! I want to try the full-moon shrimp patty.
喔！我想要試看看月亮蝦餅。

E Sure. Lily, do you want anything else?
好啊。莉莉，你還想要點些什麼嗎？

L I would like a burburchacha for my dessert!
我想要點摩摩喳喳當甜點。

A What is that? It sounds funny!
那是甚麼？聽起來很好笑。

L It's made with coconut milk and something I don't know its name.
是用椰奶跟一些我不知道名字的東西做的。

It's a famous Thai dessert.
這是很有名的泰式甜點。

E Guess we are ready to order then? Waiter!
我猜我們準備好要點餐了吧？服務生！

discuss *(v.)*	討論
portion *(n.)*	一份
patty *(n.)*	餡餅
burburchacha (泰文)	摩摩喳喳
coconut *(n.)*	椰子

Part
3

西式食物

Western Cuisine

Taipei is so fun!

義式料理 (1)
Italian Cuisine (I)

Lily is an exchange student from the U.S.A. and her classmate, Nicola, is an exchange student from Italy.

莉莉是來自美國的交換學生，而尼可拉是來自義大利的交換學生。

They are having a small talk now.

他們正在聊天。

N: Nicola 尼可拉 L: Lily 莉莉

N Hey, Lily! I heard you took Eric to a Thai restaurant.

嘿！莉莉，我聽說你跟艾利克去了一間泰式餐廳。

L Oh, you are such a nosy parker.

喔！你真是個包打聽！

Nothing can hide from you.

甚麼都逃不了你的眼睛。

N So it's true! Now I am jealous.
所以是真的囉！我現在覺得忌妒了。

L Nicola, don't be silly.
尼可拉，別傻了！

I went with Alina and Eric.
我跟艾琳娜還有艾力克一起去的！

N I know! Haha! I was teasing you.
我知道啦！哈哈！鬧著妳玩的！

My stomach feels a bit home sick today.
我的胃今天有一點想家。

L Your stomach? Homesick?
你的胃？思鄉病？

N Yeah, it's kind of missing Italian food.
對啊，它有點想想念義大利食物！

L Argh! I see. You are from Italy.
啊！我懂了！你是從義大利來的！

That's why!

所以才會這樣。

N Come on, Lily. Have Italian dinner with me.

來嘛，莉莉！跟我一起去吃義大利晚餐！

L Ha! This is what it's all about!

哈！原來一切都是為了這個啊！

關鍵單字

nosy parker *(n. phr.)*	包打聽
jealous *(adj.)*	忌妒的
tease *(v.)*	逗弄
home sick *(adj. phr.)*	想家的
Italian *(adj.)*	義大利的

• Unit 2

義式料理 (2)
Italian Cuisine (Ⅱ)

Lily is an exchange student from the U.S.A. and her classmate, Nicola, is an exchange student from Italy.

莉莉是來自美國的交換學生，而尼可拉是來自義大利的交換學生。

They are having dinner together in an Italian restaurant.

他們正在一間義式料理餐廳用晚餐。

> N: Nicola 尼可拉 L: Lily 莉莉

N Do you prefer rissoto or pasta tonight, madam?

女士，你比較想要吃義大利燉飯還是麵呢？

L Oh, I want to try both!

喔，我兩個都想要試看看耶！

N Very greedy, madam.

非常貪心啊，女士！

L Haha. You are the expert.
哈哈！你是專家。

Why don't you make some recommendation?
你何不推薦一下？

N Okay. The rissoto is a rice dish cooked in broth to a creamy consistency.
好的！燉飯是用米飯料理，用湯汁熬煮成有濃稠奶油濃度的料理。

It contains butter and onion.
含有奶油跟洋蔥。

L Wow. You do know how to cook Italian food.
哇！你真的知道怎麼煮義大利料理啊！

N Of course! I learn from my grandmom.
當然！我跟我奶奶學的！

L Cool! Did she also teach you how to make pizza, speghetti, and lasagne?
太酷了！那她有教你怎麼做披薩、義大利麵，跟千層麵嗎？

N Sure! And ravioli, tortellini, gnocchi...
對啊，還有義大利方餃、圓形肉餡餃、馬鈴薯麵疙瘩…

L Okay, okay. You make me so hungry now!
好了好了！你把我弄得好餓喔！

Does this restaurant serve those dishes?
這間餐廳有供應那些餐點嗎？

N No, just rissoto and pasta. Sorry.
沒有，只有燉飯跟通心麵。抱歉。

But they make good pesto.
但是他們的青醬做得很好。

L Then I'll have pesto rissoto.
那麼我要一份青醬燉飯。

N Good choice! I'll have the same.
選得好！我也要一樣的！

關鍵單字

risotto *(n.)*	義大利燉飯
pasta *(n.)*	義大利麵食
greedy *(adj.)*	貪心的
expert *(n.)*	專家
broth *(n.)*	肉湯、菜湯
creamy *(adj.)*	濃稠奶油的
consistency *(n.)*	濃度

• Unit 3

墨西哥料理 (1)
Mexican Cuisine (Ⅰ)

Lily is an exchange student from the U.S.A. and her classmate, Nicola, is an exchange student from Italy.
莉莉是來自美國的交換學生，而尼可拉是來自義大利的交換學生。

They are having a small talk now.
他們正在聊天。

N: Nicola 尼可拉 L: Lily 莉莉

L Nicola, how's your stomach today?
尼可拉，你的胃今天好嗎？

N Yeah. It's fine. Why?
它好好的啊！為什麼問？

L Because you said it felt home sick last time!
因為你上次説它想家啊！

N Haha! Lily, you are fun.
哈哈！莉莉，你真有趣！

L Thanks! But seriously, I feel like eating something spicy.
謝啦！但說真的，謝啦！但是我今天想吃點辣的！

How about having some Mexican cuisine?
來點墨西哥料理如何？

N No problem! I can handle jalapenos!
沒問題！我受得了墨西哥辣椒！

I happen to know a great Mexican restaurant.
我剛好知道一間很棒的墨西哥餐廳。

It's in Da-an district.
在大安區。

L Really? I don't know there's any Mexican restaurant in Taipei!
真的嗎？我不知道台北有墨西哥餐廳耶！

N Taipei is amazing, you know.
你應該要知道，台北真的很棒！

There are so various kinds of restaurants from all over the world here.
這裡有來自世界各地各種不一樣風味的餐廳。

It is a food paradise.

這裡就是美食天堂啊。

L Please take me to the Mexican restaurant!

請帶我去那間墨西哥餐廳吧！

關鍵單字

Mexican *(adj.)*	墨西哥的
jalapeno *(n.)*	墨西哥辣椒
food paradise *(n. phr.)*	美食天堂

Unit 4

墨西哥料理 (2)
Mexican Cuisine (Ⅱ)

Lily is an exchange student from the U.S.A. and her classmate, Nicola, is an exchange student from Italy.

莉莉是來自美國的交換學生，而尼可拉是來自義大利的交換學生。

They are having dinner together in a Mexican restaurant.

他們正在一間墨西哥料理餐廳用晚餐。

N: Nicola 尼可拉 L: Lily 莉莉

L Nachos! I miss nachos!
烤玉米片！我好想念烤玉米片！

N The chef is very proud of his guacamole.
這裡的廚師對酪梨醬很得意。

You can have nachos with guacamole as your starter.
你前菜可以吃烤玉米片配酪梨醬。

L OK, but I was thinking about questo.
好吧，但我剛剛本來想配起士醬。

But guacamole will do.
但酪梨醬也可以。

N What would you like for main course?
你主餐想要吃甚麼？

L Tacos, burritos, taquitos...
墨西哥玉米餅、墨西哥捲餅、烤牛肉捲…

I don't know. It is hard to decide.
我不知道，我沒辦法決定。

N Well, I can order taquitos and you choose one from tacos or burritos.
不然我點烤牛肉捲，你再從玉米餅跟捲餅裡面選一個。

Then, we share the food with each other.
然後我們一起吃。

L Nicola, you are so nice!
尼古拉，你人真好！

nachos *(n.)*	烤玉米片
guacamole *(n.)*	酪梨醬
questo *(n.)*	起士醬
taco *(n.)*	墨西哥玉米餅
burrito *(n.)*	墨西哥捲餅

• Unit 5

墨西哥料理 (3)
Mexican Cuisine (Ⅲ)

Lily is an exchange student from the U.S.A. and her classmate, Nicola, is an exchange student from Italy.

莉莉是來自美國的交換學生,而尼可拉是來自義大利的交換學生。

They are having dinner together in a Mexican restaurant.

他們正在一間墨西哥料理餐廳用晚餐。

The chef just served meals in person and said hello to Nicola.

廚師親自上菜,並且跟尼古拉打招呼。

N: Nicola 尼可拉 L: Lily 莉莉

L Nicola, how come the chef knows you?
尼古拉,廚師怎麼會認識你?

N Oh, his name is Amigo.
喔,他叫做阿米格。

My friend took me here and introduced us.

我朋友帶我來這裡，然後介紹我們認識。

L The mashed pea and the sour cream in taquitos here are absolutely incredible.

墨西哥捲餅裡的豆泥跟酸奶真得十分好吃。

N Amigo would be very pleased to hear your compliments.

阿米格聽到你的讚美會很開心的！

L Wait. You said a friend took you here.

等一下，你說有朋友帶你來這裡。

What friend? Huh?

甚麼朋友啊？

N Umm...

嗯…

關鍵單字	
taquito *(n.)*	烤牛肉捲
mashed pea *(n. phr.)*	豆泥
sour cream *(n. phr.)*	酸奶
absolutely *(adv.)*	絕對地
incredible *(adj.)*	極妙的
compliment *(n.)*	讚美

Recreation

091

PAPAGO

大自然生活

The Nature

• Unit 1

北投溫泉 (1)
Beitou Hot Springs (Ⅰ)

Judy and Gary came to Taiwan for work.
茱蒂和格瑞來台灣工作。

Now, they have lived in Taipei for three months.
現在他們已經在台北住了三個月。

J: Judy 茱蒂 G: Gary 格瑞

G What do you feel like doing tomorrow, Judy?
茱蒂，明天想要做什麼呢?

J How about going to Beitou?
去北投如何？

I heard that it is famous for soothing hot springs.
我聽說那裡有療癒性的溫泉。

G It's a good idea.
這是個好主意。

J There are many delicate hot spring resorts.

那裡有精緻的溫泉會所。

Besides, there are some art museums, too.

附近也有藝術博物館。

G Wow! Why don't we visit an art museum first and then go to take a hot spring bath?

哇！那我們先去參觀博物館再去泡溫泉，好嗎？

J Sure!

好啊。

關鍵單字

soothing *(adj.)*	療癒的	
hot spring *(n. phr.)*	溫泉	
resort *(n.)*	休閒中心	
museum *(n.)*	博物館	
take a hot spring bath *(v. phr.)*	泡溫泉澡	

• Unit 2

北投溫泉 (2)
Beitou Hot Springs (Ⅱ)

Judy and Gary are going to visit Beitou.
茱蒂跟格瑞去參觀北投。

G: Gary 格瑞 R: Reception 櫃台

G Hi, are there any brochures or pamphlets about the Beitou culture exploration tour?
你好，這裡有沒有北投文化探索行的手冊？

R Sure, here you are.
有，在這裡。

G How much is the culture exploration tour?
文化探索行要多少費用？

R NT $ 150 per person.
每人新台幣一百五十元整。

That includes the admission to museums and a guided tour.
包含入場費和導覽費。

G I see. And when does the tour start?
我知道了。旅程何時會出發？

R Our trip starts at 10 o' clock every day, except Monday.
每日十點開始，星期一除外。

G How long does a tour take?
一趟行程要花多久時間？

R It takes around two hours.
可能要花將近兩小時。

G I would likc to book a culture exploration tour for two, please.
我想要預訂這組行程，兩位。

R Not a problem.
沒問題。

關鍵單字	
brochure *(n.)*	小冊子
culture *(n.)*	文化
exploration *(n.)*	探索
tour *(n.)*	旅行
include *(v.)*	包括
admission *(n.)*	入場費
guided tour *(n. phr.)*	導覽

• Unit 3

陽明山國家公園 (1)
Yangmingshan National Park (Ⅰ)

Judy and Gary are talking about their weekend trip now.
茱蒂和格瑞正在聊他們的周末旅行。

J: Judy 茱蒂　G: Gary 格瑞

J I want to go hiking this weekend.
我這周末想去戶外走走踏青。

Any ideas?
有任何想法嗎？

G I would recommend you go to the Yangmingshan National Park.
我建議陽明山國家公園

Now, there is a flower festival.
現在那裡有花季。

We can go there and enjoy the blossom.
我們可以去那裡，欣賞繁花盛開的景象。

J Which bus shall we take?

要搭幾號公車去？

G Well, I think we can take a shuttle bus at the MRT station.

我們可以搭在捷運站的接駁車。

It will be more convenient.

那會更方便。

J How would you arrange the park tour for the flower festival?

你會如何安排參觀花季園區的行程呢？

G We can go to the information center and choose any planned activities.

我們可以去遊客中心，選擇參加設計好的活動

Or we can take a tour bus for sightseeing.

或是改搭遊園巴士遊覽。

J Have you ever heard "Yangming Shuwu", a document house there?

你有聽說過那裡有個叫做陽明書屋的地方嗎？

G It was once a summer house where the late president received guests.

那以前是個避暑場所，台灣先總統曾在那裡招待貴賓。

Later, it was refurbished as a document house in memory of him.

之後，這個屋子被改裝，以書屋的形式紀念先總統。

Now, it is a famous historical site.

現在那裡是一個知名的歷史遺跡。

關鍵單字

go hiking *(v. phr.)*	去踏青
recommend *(v.)*	推薦
flower festival *(n. phr.)*	花季
tour bus *(n. phr.)*	遊園巴士
president *(n.)*	總統
refurbish *(v.)*	裝修

094

• Unit 4

陽明山國家公園 (2)
Yangmingshan National Park (Ⅱ)

Judy and Gary are talking about their weekend trip to the Yangmingshan National Park now.

茱蒂和格瑞正在聊他們的周末陽明山國家公園之旅。

J: Judy 茱蒂 G: Gary 格瑞

G Have you heard of calla lilies?
你有聽說過海芋嗎？

J No, what is it?
沒有耶，那是什麼？

G Calla lilies are white flowers and they are beautiful.
海芋是種白花，而且很漂亮。

Bamboo Lake in the Yangmingshan National Park is well-known for these flowers.
陽明山國家公園竹子湖以海芋聞名。

I think we can go there and pick up some.

我想我們可以去那裡摘些海芋。

J That would be wonderful!
那太棒了！

Are there any activities for the night?
那晚上有活動嗎？

G And we can take a picture in front of the famous flower clock in the park as well.
我們可以在著名的花鐘前拍照。

How about going to Chinese Culture University and enjoying the night view of Taipei.
我們去文化大學看台北的夜景如何？

J I can't wait for it!
我真是期待！

關鍵單字

calla lily *(n. phr.)*	海芋
Bamboo lake *(n. phr.)*	竹子湖
take a picture *(v. phr.)*	拍照

095

• Unit 5

象山自然步道 (1)
Xiangshan Hiking Trail (I)

Judy and Gary are having breakfast
together.
茱蒂和格瑞正一起用早餐。

J: Judy 茱蒂　G: Gary 格瑞

G Judy! I find a hiking trail where people
can see the night view of Taipei.
茱蒂！我發現一條登山步道從那可以看到台
北的夜景。

J Where is it?
在哪裡？

G It's in the Xinyi District.
在信義區。

J Really? You know what it is called?
真的嗎？你知道名字嗎？

G It is called the Xiangshan Hiking Trail.
象山登山步道。

Xiangshan means elephant's mountain.
象山的意思是像大象的山。

J Then I guess its name is derived from its shape.
那我猜它的名字是源自於它的形狀。

G You are right!
答對了！

It looks like an elephant's head. That's why.
它看起來像顆大象的頭，就是這樣！

關鍵單字	
trail *(n.)*	步道
look like *(v. phr.)* 看	起來像…
elephant *(n.)*	大象

096

• Unit 6

象山自然步道 (2)
Xiangshan Hiking Trail (Ⅱ)

Judy and Gary are talking about the Xiangshan Hiking trail.
茱蒂和格瑞正聊象山步道。

J: Judy 茱蒂 G: Gary 格瑞

J How long does it take to hike the whole trail?
整條步道走完要多久？

G The length of hiking trail is 1.5 kilometers.
象山步道大約共一點五公里。

I think it will take us 140 minutes.
我想要花一個小時四十分鐘吧。

J Is there anything interesting?
那裡有什麼有趣的東西呢？

G You can look over the Xinyi District and Taipei 101 on the top of the mountain.
在山頂上，你可以縱覽信義區跟台北 101 大樓。

Moreover, the mountain is an eco-paradise itself.

此外，象山本身就是個生態樂園。

What's even better, there are many signs along the trail to guide and instruct visitors about its features.

更棒的是，步道途中有很多解說牌導引遊客認識山中特色。

Are you ready to go with me?

你準備好要跟我一起攻頂了嗎？

J I'm all ready to go.
我準備好了。

G Let's go!
那我們走吧！

關鍵單字	
eco (=ecological) *(adj.)*	生態的
paradise *(n.)*	樂園

097

•Unit 7

平溪燈會 (1)
Pingxi Lantern Festival (I)

Gary and Judy are talking about how to celebrate their first Lantern Festival in Taipei.

格瑞跟茱蒂正在聊著如何慶祝他們在台北的第一個元宵節。

G: Gary 格瑞　J: Judy 茱蒂

J What are you going to do this weekend?
這個周末你有什麼活動嗎？

G Oh, it is Lantern Festival.
喔，剛好是元宵節。

I am going to launch a sky lantern in Pingxi
我要去平溪放天燈。

J What is Lantern Festival?
元宵節是什麼？

G It is the last day of the Chinese New Year.

這是中國新年的最後一天。

People celebrate this day by carrying lanterns, solving lantern riddles, and tasting some rice balls.

人們會提燈籠，猜謎及吃湯圓來慶祝這一天。

In Taiwan, people love to go to Pingxi to launch sky lanterns on Lantern Festival.

在台灣，人們喜愛在元宵節這天去平溪放天燈。

關鍵單字

sky lantern *(n. phr.)*	天燈
celebrate *(v.)*	慶祝
riddle *(n.)*	謎語
rice ball *(n.)*	湯圓

098

·Unit 8

平溪燈會 (2)
Pingxi Lantern Festival (Ⅱ)

Gary and Judy are talking about their trip to Pingxi Lantern Festival.
格瑞跟茱蒂正在聊著他們平溪燈會之旅。

G: Gary 格瑞 J: Judy 茱蒂

J How do you get to Pingxi?
那平溪要怎麼去？

G I will take a train to Ruifang Station and then transfer to the Pingxi Line.
我會搭乘火車到瑞芳，然後再轉平溪支線。

J Launching sky lanterns is new and interesting to me.
放天燈對我而言新奇又有趣。

I want to join you to Pinxi.
我想跟你一起去平溪。

G Great! We can visit Jingtong Old Street first and then go visiting Pingxi Old Street.

太好了！我們可以先到菁桐老街，再去平溪老街。

If we still have time, we can go to see the Shifen Waterfall.

如果我們還有時間，我們可以去看看十分瀑布。

J Well, when will we launch sky lanterns?

我們什麼時候可以放天燈？

G We can do that in Pingxi Old Street.

我們可以在平溪老街放天燈。

Many shops sell sky lanterns there.

在平溪老街有許多店家售有天燈。

We can buy some lanterns and write our wishes on them.

我們可以買幾只燈籠，然後寫上祝福的話語。

J That's great!

那真是太棒了！

099

Part

2

文化生活

The Culture

Taipei is so fun!

• Unit 1

國立故宮博物院 (1)

The National Palace Museum
(Ⅰ)

Yuki is Ruby's cousin and she is a Japanese.

由紀是露比堂妹，是個日本人。

She comes to Taipei to spend her summer vacation.

她來台北過暑假。

> Y: Yuki 由紀 R: Ruby 露比

Y Hey, Ruby.

嘿，露比！

If you are going to name a must-see in Taipei, which one would you recommend?

如果要你說一個到台北必看的地方，你會推薦甚麼？

R Oh, that. I would say it should be the National Palace Museum.

喔，我會說是國立故宮博物院。

Y Why?

為什麼？

R Don't you know there are a lot of world-famous masterpieces?

你不知道嗎裡面有很多世界知名的傑作嗎。？

Y Oh! You mean the Jadeite Cabbage with Insects, right?

喔！你是說翠玉白菜，對嗎？

R Yes, and the whole building is just like a Chinese palace.

對啊，而且整棟建築就像中國的皇宮一樣。

A trip to Taipei will never be complete without a visit to the National Palace Museum.

來台北玩一定要去故宮，旅程才算完整。

關鍵單字

masterpiece *(n.)*	傑作
palace *(n.)*	皇宮
jadeite *(n.)*	硬玉

●Unit 2

國立故宮博物院 (2)
The National Palace Museum (Ⅱ)

Yuki and Ruby are planning to go to the National Palace Museum
由紀與露比計畫著要去國立故宮博物院。

Y: Yuki 由紀 R: Ruby 露比

R If you are interested, I can show you around there this weekend.
如果你有興趣的話，我這周末可以帶你去那看看。

There are some special exhibitions which interest me.
有些我有興趣的展覽。

Y Sure! I am interested in antiques, too.
好啊！我也對古代文物深感興趣。

But what's the most convenient way to get to the National Palace Museum?
那到博物館最方便的方式是什麼啊？

R I think we can take the shuttle bus 30.
我想我們可以搭 30 號接駁巴士。

It will take us about half an hour.
車程約需要半小時。

Y When is the museum open?
請問博物館何時開放呢？

R The museum is open from 08:30 to 18:30 every day all year round.
博物館全年從早上八點三十分到晚上六點半營業。

Y That's cool. I'm looking forward to it now!
太棒了，我現在就開始期待了！

關鍵單字

antiques *(n. pl.)*　　　　古文物

• Unit 3

華山文化創意產業園區 (1)

Huashan 1914 Creative Park (Ⅰ)

Judy and Frank are colleagues.
茱蒂和法蘭克是同事。

They are having a chat now.
他們正在聊天。

J: Judy 茱蒂　F: Frank 法蘭克

F What are you and Gary up to this weekend?
你和格瑞周末有什麼活動嗎？

J We are going to an exhibition in a museum or something like that.
我們計劃要去看展覽或之類的事情。

F Wow, you are so cultural!
哇，你們真有文藝氣息！

What are you going to see?
你們要看什麼展覽？

J Well, actually we do not have the slightest idea about exhibitions.
嗯，事實上我們對展覽絲毫概念都沒有。

Would you recommend something to us?
你能推薦些好展覽給我們嗎？

F Have you been to the Huashan 1914 Creative Park?
你有去過華山創意園區嗎？

There are numerous creative exhibitions on weekends.
那裡每周末都有些創意展覽。

I think you will like them.
我想你們應該會喜歡。

關鍵單字	
cultural *(adj.)*	文化的
exhibition *(n.)*	展覽
slight *(adj.)*	些微，細微

• Unit 4

華山文化創意產業園區 (2)

Huashan 1914 Creative Park (Ⅱ)

Frank is introducing the Huashan 1914 Creative Park to Judy.

法蘭克正在向介紹茱蒂華山文化創意產業園區。他們正在聊天。

J: Judy 茱蒂 F: Frank 法蘭克

F Most of the exhibitions at the Huashan 1914 Creative Park are about creativity and fine arts.

大多數在華山文化創意產業園區的展覽都是有關創意與藝術。

Some are even trendy and avant-garde.

有些甚至很潮流與前衛。

J It sounds cool.

聽起來不錯。

J Do you think I need to book tickets to exhibition there first?

你認為那裡的展覽有需要先訂票嗎?

F Yes, I think so.
我覺得有需要。

Why don't you call the ticket agency to book tickets first?
何不先打電話給購票處訂票呢？

J Thanks for your recommendation.
謝謝你提供的建議。

F Have fun.
祝你有美好的行程。

關鍵單字

fine arts *(n. phr.)*	藝術	
ticket agency *(n. phr.)*	票務代理	
recommendation *(n.)*	推薦	

103

Part 3

城市生活

The Urban Life

Taipei is so fun!

西門町 (1)
Going to Ximen Street (I)

Yuki is Ruby's cousin and she is a Japanese.

由紀是露比堂妹，是個日本人。

She comes to Taipei to spend her summer vacation.

她來台北過暑假。

Now, Yuki and Ruby are planning their day with Frank.

現在，由紀跟露比正在和法蘭克計畫他們這天要做什麼。

Y: Yuki 由紀 R: Ruby 露比 F: Frank 法蘭克

Y Hi, Ruby. What are you going to do today?

嗨，露比。你今天打算做些甚麼？

R I feel like to take a walk just to look around the city.

嗨，我想到處走走看看這個城市。

F Oh! Then you must take a look at Ximen Street.

喔! 那你一定要看看西門町。

There are a creative fair, a movie theater, and food and drink shops are everywhere.

那邊有個創意市集、電影院，而且食物和飲料的店到處都是。

R And there is a historical building called the Red House.

還有一間歷史建築，叫做紅樓。

Now it is a movie theater.

現在它是間電影院。

Y It sounds pretty good.

聽起來還不錯。

Let's go together, shall we?

我們一起去，好嗎？

關鍵單字

movie theater *(n. phr.)*　　戲院

104

•Unit 2

西門町 (2)
Going to Ximen Street (Ⅱ)

Yuki, Ruby and Frank are going to visit Ximen Street.
由紀、露比和法蘭克要去西門町逛逛。

Y: Yuki 由紀 R: Ruby 露比 F: Frank 法蘭克

Y Look at the young man!
看那個年輕人！

R Wow! His dancing moves are really great!
哇！他的舞步真的很棒耶！

F Yeah, the street performance here is famous.
對啊，這裡的街頭表演很有名。

For example, the young man here is performing the street dance.
像是這個輕人就是在表演街舞。

A guy there who looks like a samurai is doing cosplay.
那邊一個看起來像是日本武士的人就是在角色扮演。

R Here we are! The Red House is over there.
我們到囉！紅樓就在那喔！

Do you want to go to the movies?
想要去看電影嗎？

Y That's a good idea. Let's go.
好主意，走吧。

F Look at the line for the movie!
你看到那邊排隊人潮嗎！

You two wait in line here.
你們在這排隊。

I'll go to buy some Coke and popcorn.
我去買可樂及爆米花。

105

•Unit 3

百貨公司 (1)

Going Shopping at a Department Store (Ⅰ)

After the movie, Yuki, Ruby and Frank are going to go shopping.
看完電影，由紀、露比和法蘭克要去逛街。

Y: Yuki 由紀 R: Ruby 露比 F: Frank 法蘭克

Y Is there any shopping center nearby?
請這附近有購物中心嗎？

I want to buy some cosmetics.
我要買化妝品。

R Yes, there are some department stores around.
有啊，附近這邊有些百貨公司。

F How about taking a taxi to get there.
搭計程車去如何？

Y How much is the taxi fare from here to there?
從這邊到百貨公司的計程車車費要多少啊？

F About two hundred and fifty.
大約要兩百五十元整。

Y Can you tell me where the taxi stand is?
你能告訴我這邊的計程車招呼站在哪邊嗎？

R Well, we can call the service or just hail a taxi.
嗯，我們可以電話叫車或舉手招車就可以了。

關鍵單字

cosmetics *(n.)*	化妝品
taxi stand *(n. phr.)*	計程車招呼站
fare *(n.)*	車費
hail *(v.)*	招呼(計程車)

106

• Unit 4

百貨公司 (2)
Going Shopping at a Department Store (Ⅱ)

After the movie, Yuki, Ruby and Frank are going to go shopping.
看完電影，由紀、露比和法蘭克要去逛街。

Y: Yuki 由紀 R: Ruby 露比
F: Frank 法蘭克 C: Clerk 店員

C Good afternoon, madam.
小姐午安。

Welcome to Sister Department Store.
歡迎到姊妹百貨公司。

How can I help you?
有需要效勞的地方嗎？

Y Yes, I want a bottle of lotion and lipstick.
我想要買乳液及口紅。

C For dry skin or for oily skin?
請問乳液是要乾性肌膚還是油性肌膚的？

Y Do you have lotion for combination?
有混合性肌用的乳液嗎？

C Yes. How about this one?
有的，這組好嗎？

Y That is fine. Thank you.
謝謝，那這組應該可以。

Could you wrap it up, please?
可以幫我打包嗎？

C Sure. Here you go.
沒問題，東西在這邊。

It's NT $ 3,000.
一共要新台幣三千元整。

Y Thank you.
謝謝你。

關鍵單字

lotion *(n.)*	乳液
lipstick *(n.)*	唇膏
wrap *(v.)*	打包

107

Unit 5

百貨公司 (3)

Going Shopping at a Department Store (Ⅲ)

After the movie, Yuki, Ruby and Frank are shopping at a department store.
看完電影，由紀、露比和法蘭克正在一間百貨公司逛逛。

Y: Yuki 由紀 R: Ruby 露比
F: Frank 法蘭克 C: Clerk 店員

R Umm... Do you know where the women's clothing section is?
呃…你知道是女裝部在哪嗎？

C It is on the 2nd floor.
女裝部在二樓。

Go straight along the aisle, and you will find the elevator to the 2nd floor.
沿著走道，你就會找到上二樓的電梯。

R Thank you.
謝謝你。

They are at the women's clothing section.
他們在女裝部。

C May I help you?
有需要效勞的地方嗎？

R I'm looking for a skirt to match my blouse.
我想要找件能搭配我上衣的裙子。

C You may want to try on the skirt.
你或許會想試試這件裙子。

R Do you have larger size?
你們有比較大的尺寸嗎？

C Yes. I will get you one.
有的，我等會拿給你。

關鍵單字	
match *(v.)*	搭配
blouse *(n.)*	女用襯衫

服飾用語

內衣 underwear

內褲 underpants

汗衫 undershirt

男用四角褲 boxers

毛衣 sweater

運動短褲 trunks

背心 vest

內搭褲 leggings

毛皮大衣 fur coat

牛仔褲 jeans

皮夾克 leather jacket

長褲 trousers

運動套頭上衣 jumper

短褲 shorts

兩件式上衣 twinset

裙子 skirt

睡衣 pajama

襪子 socks

雨衣 raincoat

皮帶 belt

孕婦裝 maternity clothes

領帶 tie

連帽 T 恤 hoody

鈕扣 button

108

• Unit 6

相機街 (1)

Looking for a New Camera in Camera Street (I)

Yuki and Ruby are having a small talk now.

由紀和露比正在聊天。

Y: Yuki 由紀　R: Ruby 露比

Y My camera doesn't work.
我的相機故障了。

Where can I get this camera repaired?
請問哪裡可修相機呢？

R You can take it to Camera Street.
你可以到相機街去檢查看看。

Y Camera street?
相機街？

R Yes. It is located in Hankou Street and Bo'ai Street.
是的，位於漢口街與博愛街。

The street is famous for the camera shops there.

那條街以相機店聞名。

Ⓡ Take your broken camera.

帶著你故障的相機。

Let's go there together.

我們一起去吧。

關鍵單字

camera *(n.)*		相機
repaired *(adj.)*		被修理的

• Unit 7

相機街 (2)

Looking for a New Camera in Camera Street (Ⅱ)

Yuki and Ruby are going to Camera Street to have a camera fixed.
由紀和露比要去相機街修相機。

Y: Yuki 由紀 R: Ruby 露比 C: Clerk 店員

C There is something wrong with the shutter.
快門出了問題。

Y Can you repair it?
你能修好它嗎？

C I'm not sure. I will do my best.
不能確定，但我盡力完成。

R: How long will it take?
修理要多久時間？

C About one hour.
大概要一個小時。

Y How much does it cost?
修理要花多少費用？

I hope it's not too expensive
我希望不要太貴。

C It might cost you NT $ 1,000.
可能要花1000元。

R That's affordable.
還負擔的起。

關鍵單字	
shutter *(n.)*	快門
affordable *(adj.)*	負擔得起

• Unit 8

相機街 (3)

Looking for a New Camera in Camera Street (Ⅲ)

An hour later, Yuki and Ruby are going to take the camera in a shop at Camera Street.

一小時之後，由紀和露比要去相機街店裡拿相機。

Y: Yuki 由紀 R: Ruby 露比 C: Clerk 店員

Y Hi, is my camera fixed?
嗨，我的相機修好了嗎？

C Yes, here you are.
是的，在這裡。

Have you ever thought about getting a new one?
有考慮要換一台新的相機嗎？

Y Yeah. I've been thinking about it.
有啊，我有考慮。

C Well, how about this? The latest one?
嗯，那這台呢？最新的款式？

It is very user-friendly and thinner size.
它非常好操作又輕巧。

R Is this a digital camera?
是數位相機嗎？

C Yes, it is and it can focus automatically.
是的，而且這台可以自動對焦。

Y If my old one is out of order again, I'll get a new one from you.
如果我這台舊的再故障的話，我就來你這買新的。

關鍵單字

user-friendly *(adj.)*	友善的
thinner *(adj.)*	輕巧的
digital *(adj.)*	數位的
automatically *(adv.)*	自動地

Unit 9

光華商場
Guang Hua Digital Plaza

Yuki and Ruby are having a small talk now.
由紀和露比正在聊天。

Y: Yuki 由紀 R: Ruby 露比

Y I have heard that Taiwan is famous for its 3C industry.
我聽說台灣以 3C 產業聞名。

R Yeah, and you can get all 3C products and parts in the Guang Hua Digital Plaza.
是啊，你可以在光華商場賣到所有的 3C 商品與零件。

It is Taipei's "3C paradise".
那是台北的 3C 天堂。

Y Any shops you recommend?
你有建議的店家嗎？

R No. I think you'd better get there in person to look for things you want.

沒有，我想你最好親自去現場找你想要的東西。

Y Will clerks there help install software for free?

店員會免費幫忙安裝軟體嗎？

R Well, it depends.

嗯，這要看店家了。

But I think you have to check the product you want carefully by yourself.

但我想你要自己仔細檢查你要買的商品。

關鍵單字	
assemble *(v.)*	組裝
computer *(n.)*	電腦
parts *(n. pl.)*	零件
install *(v.)*	安裝

永續圖書
線上購物網

www.foreverbooks.com.tw

◆ 加入會員即享活動及會員折扣。

◆ 每月均有優惠活動，期期不同。

◆ 新加入會員三天內訂購書籍不限本數金額，
   即贈送精選書籍一本。（依網站標示為主）

專業圖書發行、書局經銷、圖書出版

永續圖書總代理：

五觀藝術出版社、培育文化、棋茵出版社、犬拓文化、讀
品文化、雅典文化、知音人文化、手藝家出版社、瓊申文
化、智學堂文化、語言鳥文化

活動期內，永續圖書將保留變更或終止該活動之權利及最終決定權。

台北PAPAGO！跟老外介紹台北

雅致風靡　典藏文化

親愛的顧客您好，感謝您購買這本書。即日起，填寫讀者回函卡寄回至本公司，我們每月將抽出一百名回函讀者，寄出精美禮物並享有生日當月購書優惠！想知道更多更即時的消息，歡迎加入 "永續圖書粉絲團" 您也可以選擇傳真、掃描或用本公司準備的免郵回函寄回，謝謝。

傳真電話：（02）8647-3660　　　　電子信箱：yungjiuh@ms45.hinet.net

姓名：		性別：　□男　　□女
出生日期：　　年　　月　　日		電話：
學歷：		職業：
E-mail：		
地址：□□□		
從何處購買此書：		購買金額：　　　　元

購買本書動機：□封面 □書名□排版 □內容 □作者 □偶然衝動

你對本書的意見：
內容：□滿意□尚可□待改進　　編輯：□滿意□尚可□待改進
封面：□滿意□尚可□待改進　　定價：□滿意□尚可□待改進

其他建議：

總經銷：永續圖書有限公司

永續圖書線上購物網
www.foreverbooks.com.tw

您可以使用以下方式將回函寄回。

您的回覆，是我們進步的最大動力，謝謝。

① 使用本公司準備的免郵回函寄回。

② 傳真電話：（02）8647-3660

③ 掃描圖檔寄到電子信箱：

　　yungjiuh@ms45.hinet.net

- -

沿此線對折後寄回，謝謝。

　2 2 1 - 0 3

雅典文化事業有限公司　收

新北市汐止區大同路三段194號9樓之1

雅致風靡　典藏文化